D0984984

DEAD MAN ON A BLACK HORSE

GUILTY. The verdict had been handed down and the sentence pronounced. The mob in the jailyard was hungry for blood ... Jim Shay was railroaded straight into a lynching, and the only way he could prove he wasn't a killer was by turning outlaw.

A condemned prisoner escapes his guards on the way to the penitentiary and begins a desperate ride across treacherous, Indian-infested desert ... as he hunts down a band of cut-throats led by the most vicious female in the West, a dance-hall girl with a dangerous greed for gold.

DEAD MAN ON A BLACK HORSE

Ray Hogan

HOG

First published 1966

This hardback edition 1997
by Chivers Press
by arrangement with
Golden West Literary Agency

Copyright © 1966 by Ray Hogan
Copyright © 1968 by Ray Hogan in the British
Commonwealth
Copyright © renewed 1994 by Ray Hogan
All rights reserved

ISBN 0 7451 8934 2

For Lois

British Library Cataloguing in Publication Data available

Printed and bound in Great Britain by
Redwood Books, Trowbridge, Wiltshire

OCT 1997

1

A hot, powder-dry wind blew in gusts through Sacramento Springs. It swept down the main street, picking up the last of winter's dead leaves along with bits of trash, and hurried it all toward the river in small, spinning dust devils. Jim Shay, standing at the window of his cell, watched in sullen bitterness.

Abruptly he jerked away and swore deeply. For over a week he had been cooped up in this stinking jail—all of that miserable time, except for a couple of hours given over to the trial, had been spent in this 6 by 8 foot cage. The confinement was killing him—just as surely as those bastards on the jury were out to kill him.

Somewhere in the thin scatter of buildings huddled together on the flat edging the Rio Grande, a church bell began to thud dully. Immediately a dog barked, as though objecting to the slow, metallic sound. Shay wondered if the tolling had anything to do with him.

Earlier the jury had retired to consider its decision; maybe this meant the decision had been reached, and the bell was a signal for the blood-hungry vultures of Sacramento Springs to gather around.

They could guess again if they thought they were going to hang him. They couldn't have found him guilty—not on the evidence produced and the testimony given by that deputy, Gilman. Anyone with a thimbleful of brains could see that it

7

was all circumstantial, that it had just been luck he happened to be at the Slausson place when the deputy rode up.

But big Rue Gilman was the sort of man to whom you couldn't tell anything; that two-bit star he wore gave him leave to figure out things the way he wanted, and to hell with what had actually taken place.

A chair scraped against the floor in the front of the jail where the sheriff maintained his office. The hollow beat of boot heels followed. The bell had meant something, sure enough. Shay faced the hallway. They were coming for him —and now he would know.

The door opened. Sheriff George Cole and his two deputies, Gilman and the still-faced Mexican, Miguel Sierra, stepped into the narrow runway fronting the cells.

"All right," Cole said in his dry, impersonal way, "the judge's ready. Unlock the door, Rue."

Gilman, his moon-shaped, ruddy face serious, moved to the grating. He wore two cross-belted guns around his ample belly, and for a fleeting instant Jim Shay entertained the idea of grabbing one and making a run for it. It would be a fool stunt. Sierra, cool, withdrawn, and completely efficient, lounged in the doorway, one hand resting on the butt of his pistol. And George Cole, for all his years, was no greenhorn, either.

"You heard the sheriff—move!" Gilman snapped, grasping Shay's arm.

Jim wrenched free and spun about, his eyes glittering. "Keep your hands off me, you son of a bitch!" he snarled.

The big deputy drew back. His face darkened and his mouth pulled down into a hard-cornered, expectant smile. Cole, calm and in full control, stepped between the two men.

"Never mind," he said firmly in a quiet voice.

Shay, simmering with anger, stepped into the corridor. Cole moved up to his left. They walked the length of the passageway and out into the dazzling sunlight of the street. Immediately Rue Gilman, determined as always to be in the fore, closed in on Shay's right. Sierra brought up the rear.

Jim shuttled a glance to Cole. "Any point in me asking what the jury decided?"

"No point," the lawman replied laconically.

Gilman laughed. "Hell—ain't no doubt in your mind, is there?"

Shay gave the deputy's overlarge, overdressed bulk a withering look. "Where you're concerned, I reckon not."

Gilman had really nailed him to the wall during the trial. When the deputy was put on the stand he had come up with things that had nothing to do with the crime, yet he had managed to make them appear damaging and conclusive evidence. Twice when the prosecutor was on thin ice, endeavoring to tie in some inconsequential bit of information, Gilman had managed to suddenly remember facts that clinched the matter for the floundering lawyer. He owed the deputy plenty, Jim thought harshly. . . . And someday . . . when he got the chance. . . .

The street was almost deserted; practically all of the settlement had gathered in the courtroom by now. A half a dozen or so men, defying the blistering heat, lounged in front of Cook's General Store. They watched the small procession with flat, expressionless eyes. They would be members of the Vengadors, Jim guessed, and they also awaited the verdict with interest.

Their name defined their calling: self-appointed lawmen, a vigilance committee. Once they had been necessary, when law enforcement was a scarce commodity in the territory, but times had changed and there was now no need for on-the-spot trial and execution. The Vengadors, however, chose not to recognize that fact.

Shay felt their surly gazes upon him as he mounted the steps of the DeBaca Hotel, where the courtroom, consisting of two adjoining rooms, upper front, was located. Pocketed by the three lawmen, he crossed the porch and entered the lobby. Here were more men, and they all turned silently to watch him, in that close, fixed manner of those spewing their hatred upon a man already convicted in their narrow minds, and slated, insofar as they were concerned, for the gallows.

Jim Shay favored them with a hard, contemptuous stare, followed Cole up the stairs and down the hall to a door at its far end. The sheriff flung the varnished panel open and ushered Shay into the stifling, crowded room, heavy with the odors of smoke, sweat, and disturbed dust. The jurymen were in their places, but their solemn expressions gave him no clue as to their decision.

"Everybody up!"

The clerk of the court, sweating profusely in his blue serge suit, high celluloid collar, and bow tie, spoke out sharply.

There was a noisy clatter of chairs. The Honorable Amos McGrath, judge of the district, entered. To Jim Shay, McGrath was still somewhat of a mystery; he wasn't sure whether the judge was a crusader honestly endeavoring to improve and strengthen the status of the law—or a politician striving for a higher position.

McGrath was young for the job, no more than forty, and he tried to assume the appearance of age by affecting a pointed beard and wearing steel-rimmed, pince-nez spectacles. His jaw was set now to a determined angle, and his thin, almost white brows became vertical lines as he took his position behind the oak table that served as his bench.

Again chairs clattered and clothing rustled as spectators, jurymen, and court officials resumed their seats. Miguel Sierra closed the door to the hallway quietly. Immediately a strained voice gasped: "My God, Sierra—leave that damn door open!"

Sierra looked at Cole. The sheriff relayed the glance to the judge. McGrath drew his brows together further, nodded across the room. Outside, in one of the fields beyond the houses, a meadowlark began to whistle, the sweet, clear notes strangely out of place in this grim room.

McGrath fixed his glance on the clerk. "You will read the charge again."

The hush deepened. The clerk rose to his feet. He ran a forefinger inside his collar to free his Adam's apple, cleared his throat. Shay, the muscles of his lean jaw bulging, waited.

"On this day of July twelfth, the year 1870, you, James Shay, are hereby charged with the murder of one Peter Slausson and wife, Amy Slausson, residents of this county, southern portion. The said murder taking place at the residence of the aforementioned parties, where you did enter, brutally beat, and subsequently kill—"

"We know all that," a voice shouted unexpectedly from the audience. "Come on, Judge—let's get started with the hangin'!"

McGrath's pale eyes flashed. He motioned to Cole. "Get that man out of here, Sheriff."

The lawman rose quickly, moved among the chairs, and halted beside the offender. "You know better'n that, Jesse. Now, get out."

The impatient Jesse got to his feet, muttered something under his breath, and slouched to the doorway. He said more to Sierra, who gave him an impassive stare, and disappeared into the hall.

"Any more such outbursts," McGrath said sternly, "and I'll clear this courtroom." He swept the crowd with his glance, allowed the words to have their effect, and then nodded to the clerk.

". . . subsequently kill the above-mentioned parties," the clerk resumed. He paused again, gulped. "To these charges the defendant pleaded not guilty."

McGrath said, "Thank you, Mr. Clerk." He turned to the jury. "On his behalf you will recall that the defendant stated he was en route to a neighboring state. He further stated that he came upon the scene of the murders after they were committed; that there was a witness to this—a man driving a wagon and a team of mules who arrived at the Slausson farm at approximately the same time as the defendant.

"The defendant was not able to name this witness nor was he able to produce him, although the lawyer appointed by the court to defend James Shay advised me that every effort was made to locate such party."

Abruptly angered, Shay leaped to his feet. "Well, he was there! I don't give a damn what they say—he was there. I've got my doubts whether they looked very hard for him."

Cole was up and moving toward him. Shay glanced at the old lawman, stifled his anger, and sat down. Cole turned back.

McGrath studied Jim coldly, then resumed. "The testimony of Deputy Sheriff Rue Gilman, who had gone to the scene of the crime at the suggestion of a passing stagecoach driver who had heard shooting in the vicinity of the Slausson place, was that he found James Shay in the Slausson house. A pistol was in his hand. Deputy Sheriff Gilman did not see anyone else—particularly not the man driving the team of mules, whose presence has been claimed by the defendant."

McGrath paused. "Now, those are the facts as brought out in the trial. Some are pertinent, others are not, and because of that I thought it best to review them in order that all concerned with this matter will have it clearly defined in their minds." He settled his eyes on the attorney selected to defend Shay. "Mr. Davis, have I omitted anything?"

Jim glanced at Davis. The lawyer had been of no help at all, accepting the appointment only because he feared to antagonize McGrath. He sat now in his chair, slumped forward, hands folded in his lap. If he had made any attempt to locate the old man with the team of black mules, it was news to Shay.

"No, your Honor." Davis mumbled.

McGrath swung to Jim. "You will rise and face the jury."

Shay got to his feet slowly. He allowed his eyes to run over the sweaty, hostile faces tipped up to him, to hesitate briefly on the smirking moon that was Rue Gilman's.

"Mr. Foreman," he heard McGrath say. "In the light of these facts, how do you find th—"

"Guilty!" the juryman shouted before the jurist had completed his question.

The reply hit Shay with solid force. He had expected it all along, yet deep in his mind had lain a belief that somehow he would be found innocent. Fury raced through him. Goddam it—he *was* innocent! And according to all the rules and the ordinary conception of justice, his innocence should have been established. Wild resentment welled up within him. Seemingly from a great distance, he heard McGrath speak again.

"Remain standing. . . ."

"The hell with that!" Jim shouted. "I never killed those people. And there's a witness who'll—"

"You have been found guilty as charged." McGrath's cold voice cut into his words. "The court is prepared to pass sentence at this time." The judge paused, waited for Shay to quiet himself, and then looked out over the courtroom.

"Before this is done there is something I want to say. There is in this area a certain group of men who have taken it upon themselves to become guardians of the law—a vigilance committee, if you will. I take this opportunity to warn them that I will tolerate no interference by them in the dispensing of justice in this matter before the court.

"I hereby charge the sheriff of this county with the responsibility of protecting the prisoner at all costs. I want that last thoroughly understood—at all costs. I trust the court has made itself clear."

There was a low rumble in the room. A hoarse voice whispered, "By God, he ain't hangin' him!" George Cole rose to his full height, swept the crowd with his hard blue eyes. The murmuring ceased. In the subsequent hush Jim could hear his heart pounding. It was unbelievable. He had been found guilty of a crime he had not committed . . . and now he was facing a judge, waiting to hear his sentence.

"James Shay"—McGrath's dispassionate tone rubbed him, dug into his consciousness— "You have been found guilty of the crime with which you were charged, and it becomes the duty of this court to pronounce sentence upon you. The court is mindful of one thing—that there was no clear-cut evidence of murder—and this factor weighs heavily upon my decision as to a just and fair punishment."

Shay's muscles tensed. He cast a sideward glance at the windows, no more than a half a dozen steps to his right. Beyond them he could see the slanted roof of the hotel's porch, and below it by ten feet or so, the street.

"It is the judgment of this court," McGrath droned on, "that you be escorted to the Territorial Penitentiary at Santa Fe, where you will be confined and serve out the balance of your natural life at hard labor."

A concerted yell of disappointment lifted in the stuffy room. In that same fragment of time something exploded within Jim Shay. Never before in his twenty-six years of life had he felt so completely helpless.

He half turned as the burst of noes grew in volume. He saw George Cole pushing his way toward him through the now standing audience. Beyond the sheriff Rue Gilman beamed proudly. Shay wheeled, leaped across the intervening space, and plunged through the window, carrying glass and framework with him.

2

He realized his impulsive act was a mistake the instant his feet touched the slanting roof of the porch. He would never make it. Off-balance, he went to his knees and rolled over the edge. Glass splinters stinging his face and hands, he struck the hard, sunbaked earth on his left shoulder. Jarred by the impact, and the yelling inside the hotel ringing in his ears, he staggered to his feet and looked wildly about. The tight knot of men in front of Cook's had come to life and were moving toward him.

He spun on his heel. There would be horses behind the hotel, in the stable. He didn't know what Cole had done with his black gelding, probably placed him in the town livery barn, but there was a slim chance he had been quartered in the stable maintained by the hostelry for its patrons' animals. If the black wasn't there, he'd borrow another.

He started for the passageway that ran between the hotel and the building adjacent to it. The angry shouts of the men rushing up from Cook's had become loud and threatening. At that moment Miguel Sierra burst from the lobby of the hotel and onto the porch. He halted, pistol in hand. Shay's hopes sagged. The Mexican had made it to the ground floor almost as quickly as he.

"No, *señor*," the deputy warned. "Behind you—look."

Shay whirled again. The Vengadors, faces grim, were almost upon him. Several had drawn their weapons; another was trotting up with a coil of rope.

"Come to me—here," Sierra said in a quick, clipped way. "There will be trouble."

Shay, cursing bitterly, veered toward the crouched figure of the deputy. George Cole and Gilman appeared in the doorway and rushed to Sierra's side.

"Stand back—all of you!" Cole shouted, moving ahead to place himself between Shay and the advancing men.

The Vengadors slowed. More men poured out of the hotel, fanning out into a thick half circle around Shay and the lawmen. The atmosphere was tense, overcharged. Only a spark was needed to set off a bloody explosion.

"Let 'em alone, George," a man yelled from the crowd. "Let 'em hang the son of a bitch! That's what he's got comin'—not just settin' around takin' it easy the rest of his life."

Cole's arm came up. Sunlight glinted off the pistol in his hand. The dusty, heatladen canyon between the false-fronted buildings echoed with the blast of a gunshot.

"I'm warning you," the lawman shouted into the abrupt silence. "Next time I won't be pointing in the air. Now, I want you back—out of the way. I'm taking my prisoner to the jail. Any man who tries to stop me's in for trouble."

The lawman motioned curtly to Sierra and Gilman. "Let's go."

Gilman laid his ham-sized hand on Shay's shoulder and gave him a rough shove. It caught Jim off-balance. He stumbled and went to one knee.

"Look out!" someone on the porch cried.

But Shay had seen Gilman closing in fast. He tried to throw himself to one side. Gilman hit him, sending him sprawling onto the splintery planking of the porch.

A red haze swirling about him, growling curses, Jim Shay leaped to his feet. That bastard of a Gilman—there was no need. . . . He lunged at the deputy. A yell rose from the crowd. Gilman, eyes alight, grinning wickedly, went for Shay. Miguel Sierra now moved in and blocked the chopping blow. The Mexican said nothing, merely faced Gilman, his dark features set and filled with a cool warning.

The deputy stood still. Shay, hate consuming him, shouldered Sierra aside. Jim smashed a hard right into Gilman's flaccid face, which sent him stumbling back into the arms of the crowd.

Shay, blind to all else, rushed forward. The yelling about him increased, but he scarcely heard it.

Strong hands suddenly seized Shay's arms and jerked him around. Miguel Sierra's voice hissed in his ear, "They have you, *amigo*. Stop now!"

Heaving, Shay hesitated. He raised his eyes as the truth of the statement penetrated his seething brain. The men in the street were at the edge of the porch. George Cole held them back only by the threat of his gun—and that he would be unable to do much longer.

A hush settled over the crowd. "Gilman . . . Sierra." Cole's voice was sharp. "Get him across to the jail. Lock him up. Nobody'll try stopping you. Nobody had better."

"Go," Sierra murmured, and pushed Shay gently off the porch.

Jim stalked into the center of the road. The Mexican stayed close to his shoulder. Behind him he could hear Gilman shouting to the men on the porch, a cursing reply to the ribbing he was taking as a result of the staggering blow Shay had delivered.

Cole eased off the board platform, his pistol drifting back and forth over the knot of sullen men. Gilman caught up and fell in with Shay and Sierra. They angled for the jail, fifty feet distant and on the opposite side of the street.

George Cole, a promise in his cold eyes, moved in between them and the glowering Vengadors. There was no bravado in the old lawman's makeup, no desire to display his courage and contempt; only a determination to conduct his prisoner to where he would be comparatively safe.

The crowd on the porch remained silent, and the street became a hushed, heated vacuum in which the four men moved warily around one cluster of threatening bystanders while a second, larger group looked on breathlessly.

They reached the sagging wooden sidewalk. Cole stepped up onto it, deliberate and careful. He was like a hunter endeavoring, with the greatest care, to give an angry, posed grizzly a wide berth, fearing each moment to make a wrong move.

They gained the entrance to the jail. Cole halted two steps from the opening. From the corner of his mouth, he said, "For

Christ's sake—get him in there—quick!" Sweat stood out on his face in huge beads, and there was a whiteness about his thin lips.

Sierra prodded Shay with his gun barrel. Jim stepped through the doorway into the close room. Gilman immediately crowded by, hurried down the corridor, and opened the inner door to the runway. He swung back the grating of the first cell, then blocked the opening with his massive shape.

"Damn you—if you ever—"

Jim Shay pushed up close to the deputy. His eyes became slits. "If I ever get the chance," he cut in, "I'll kill you, Gilman! You lied me into this. I won't be forgetting."

The big deputy stiffened. Sierra moved in again and placed himself between the two men. He motioned for Jim to enter the cell, quietly hustling Gilman away from the door. From the street George Cole's voice sounded along the corridor.

"I'll stand for nobody closer'n fifty feet."

Sierra slammed the grating and turned the lock. A faint sigh slipped from him as he looked between the bars.

"We have the good luck, *amigo*," he murmured, and maneuvering Gilman ahead of him, walked into the corridor and closed the door.

3

Shay stood in the center of his cell, impatience boiling through him. He was oblivious to the sweat that bathed his body, dampened his clothing, and beaded his gullied face; he was aware only of one thing—he was still a prisoner.

He swore and turned to the small window high in the south wall of the cage. From it he could see a short stretch of the street. The good citizens—damn their bloody souls—were still out there, hoping, no doubt, that the Vengadors would soon take over.

He had played right into their hands—almost, he thought grimly. If George Cole hadn't been the tough, no-nonsense, no-quarter lawman he was, they likely would have had him swinging from a cottonwood at this very moment. The same went for Miguel Sierra. But Gilman was something else. If the big deputy had his way he would as soon turn him over to the vigilantes as go to the privy. More so, probably.

His attempt to escape had been a fool stunt. But the reason behind it remained; the bearded old man and his team of mules must be found.

Maybe Sacramento Springs and the law weren't really interested in locating him. It certainly seemed that they only wanted satisfaction for the deaths of the Slaussons—and never mind whether the right man was being punished or no.

A fresh anger raced through Jim Shay. He whirled from the window and crossed the dusty floor of his cell to the grating. Seizing the bars, he shook them violently. By God, those bastards had better watch him close when they took him to Santa Fe. He sure as hell wasn't about to spend the rest of his life behind bars—not when the proof of his innocence was running around out there somewhere, perhaps no more than a couple of dozen miles away.

The door into the corridor opened suddenly. George Cole appeared. He paused in the rectangle briefly, then, followed by Gilman and Sierra, neared Shay's cell.

"Thanks to you and that damn judge," he said sourly, "we got one devil of a mess on our hands."

"Nobody's throwing me in the pen for something I didn't do." Shay flared. "You know damn well what the truth of this thing is."

Cole looked up. "What's the truth? How do you know when you hear it? You lay it all out in front of twelve men and they take their pack. Only way I know to find it—and far as I'm concerned, it's been done."

"Takes twelve *honest* men," Shay said coldly. "There's where you're making your mistake."

Cole shrugged. "Neither here nor there now. And you're just making it tough on all of us. Get smart, Shay. Wait until you get to Santa Fe, then start things working if you figure you've been handed a bad deal."

"From inside the pen? Who the hell you guying, Sheriff? I've heard how they treat a man there. Once you're in, you can forget there's a world outside the walls."

The lawman moved his shoulders again. "Suit yourself, mister. My job only calls for me to get you there alive. Reckon that's all I'm going to worry about."

He turned, looked at Sierra. "We're fools if we think we can keep him here tonight, so I reckon the smart thing is get him out quick. Get some of them old clothes we got hanging in the closet—some that'll fit him."

Sierra moved away without question to do the lawman's bidding, but Gilman, frowning, said, "What've you got in mind, George?"

"Just playing it safe. They come after him tonight, he won't be here. I don't want nobody hurt—not over him, anyway."

Sierra returned, carrying a shirt, pants, and a well-worn black hat. "These will fit, I think."

Cole nodded. "Open up the cell, Rue," he said. He stepped up close to Shay. "Now, listen good, mister. Do exactly what you're told—and no tricks. I'm trying my damndest to keep you from getting yourself lynched, but I don't aim to shoot any of my local people over it. You try making another break and you'll find yourself swinging in the wind."

Jim nodded. The trail to Sante Fe ran for a hundred miles—and on it lay his best chances for escape.

He pulled back as Sierra entered the cage and tossed the clothing onto the cot. Cole motioned to Shay. "Peel off. Put on that stuff Miguel brought. Give him yours."

As Jim began to undress, the old lawman looked at Gilman. "Rue, we're not waiting for dark. You're taking him out of here soon as he's ready."

"Now?" the deputy protested.

"Now," Cole echoed. "Most everybody in town's out front. I'll keep them there. You skip out the back door and get some horses. Hide them in the alley—better use that old shed behind the Crossman place. Expect you ought to throw some grub in your saddlebags. You won't be near any houses where you can eat."

"Be some farms along the way—"

"You won't be traveling the main road. You take Shay across the fields and get on the old Mesa del Oro Trail. Figure if you push right along you can make it to the Ladrones by dark. Make your camp there."

"Goddam the luck," Gilman muttered, plainly not happy about it. "What'll you be doing?"

"I'll be doing my best to keep those lynch-happy bastards busy out front. Sierra'll be wearing Shay's clothes. I aim to leave the doors open, to keep him standing at this end of the cell so's they can see him from the street. Meantime I'll drop word I'm taking him north in the morning on the stage. You get the idea?"

Sierra, finished dressing, nodded. "Sí, I understand, Sheriff."

Jim looked on silently, thinking about the trip to Santa Fe. Although he was fairly familiar with the country, the little-used back trail sounded new to him. Apparently it lay to the west, somewhere near the Ladrones, a short but wild and rugged chain of mountains that lifted above the mesa not far beyond the ordinarily dry river called the Rio Salado.

"Appears to me I'm taking a mighty long chance," Gilman said, objection still riding his tone. "Pulling out of here in broad daylight—"

"Just what nobody'll be expecting," Cole replied. He looked down and wagged his head. "Wish to hell it was the other way around—that you was the same size as him and not Miguel."

The big deputy bristled. He said, "I'll get him there, don't you worry none about that."

"Don't aim to," the sheriff said. "Once you're out of town, it'll be up to you. I'll have my hands full right here."

Gilman scratched at his jaw. "Ain't been on the Trail in quite a spell. You reckon I'm liable to run into Apaches?"

"Not likely. Been no reports of them on this side of the river. All we've heard about is what's happening on the other side of the Jornada. Soldiers at Craig's probably got them in hand now, anyway. You just bear down on leaving town without being seen. Once you've done that, you're safe."

"Ain't worried about being safe . . . Just like to know for sure how to figure things."

"It's all figured for you," Cole said wearily. "Now, get after those horses—and be careful. Don't talk to nobody, and don't let nobody see you. Understand?"

Gilman grunted as he moved toward the rear door of the building. Cole swung his attention to Sierra; he looked him over critically.

"You'll pass for him, no doubt about it. Just keep your face turned the other way."

Sierra nodded. He took up a position at the end of the cell. From there he was on a direct line, down the hallway and through the two doors, with the street. Anyone glancing in could see him standing behind the thick bars.

Cole faced Jim Shay next. "I'm saying it again—if you're smart you'll string along with this and not kick up a row. It's your neck I'm trying to save. Stick out your hands."

Jim did as directed. The lawman snapped a pair of steel, chain-linked cuffs about his wrists. "Now keep out of sight," he said. "I'm going back up front. Need to keep them standing there."

Cole stepped into the runway, slamming and locking the

grating. Shay leaned against the wall of bars opposite Sierra, who watched him with quiet indifference.

"Expect I ought to be thanking you for out there in the street," he said. "I don't feel much like thanking anybody, however, position I'm in."

Sierra smiled. "*Por nada*," he murmured. "Maybe it is Gilman who should make thanks. You would have killed him, I think."

"You can bet on it . . . "

"And so would they have killed you then, too. You have the hot head, *amigo*."

"Wouldn't you be a mite riled in my boots? They're pinning something on me that I don't have coming—mostly on account of what that fat bastard said. But this little fandango's not over with yet. I'll square things before we ever reach Santa Fe."

Sierra pulled a sack of tobacco and fold of papers from his pocket. Selecting a thin brown sheet, he tapped a quantity of the grains into a paper trough and rolled himself a thin smoke. He tossed the sack to Shay.

"I know nothing except you go to the penitentiary," he said, striking a match and holding it to the tip of the cylinder. "The law has said this. It is a job also of mine to see that it is done. Maybe you are innocent, and maybe you do all this for show. I do not know. But I will tell you this, *amigo*." He paused, exhaled a cloud of smoke, and tossed away the match. "Rue Gilman is no *tonto*—no big fool. He will give you no chance. He will kill you quick if you anger him."

Jim returned the sack of makings, studied the cigarette between his thumb and forefinger. "He'll never get me to Santa Fe," he said in a low voice. "You can lay odds on it."

Sierra shifted his position, slid a casual glance toward the street. George Cole's voice had risen as he lashed the crowd.

"Any man tries to get inside my jail is asking for a bullet. I'm taking my prisoner to Santa Fe on the morning stage—and I'm taking him alive. Now, be thinking that over if any of you are hatching ideas about coming after him . . . . "

"The old *lobo*," Sierra said softly. "He is the wise one."

Shay stirred restlessly. Maybe Cole was looking out for himself just as much as he was for his prisoner. The lawman didn't want the stigma of having lost his charge—no man would. And, too, he didn't want the blood of any townsmen on his hands. That was what was uppermost in his mind—not the value of his prisoner's life.

Jim drew himself upright, and mopped at the sweat on his cheeks. The heat was oppressive, and the clothes Sierra had given him were a bit tight. He began to fumble with the buttons of the coarse shirt. He could still hear Cole's voice and the questions being shouted at him.

"It is good for all that you will not be here this night," the Mexican said thoughtfully.

Shay started to answer, but the rear door opened just then. Gilman appeared, his heavy face gleaming with sweat. His spurs jingled loudly as he strode into the runway and passed on down the corridor to the front. He said something to George Cole, who wheeled about and reentered the building. They conversed in low voices for several moments, then doubled back to the cells. Gilman unlocked the grating; he jerked his head at Shay.

"Let's go, jailbird."

The deputy was grim-faced and spoke shortly. It was clear he did not relish the task ahead of him.

Jim stepped into the runway. Cole, closing the door so that they could not be seen from the street, handed a small key to the deputy.

"Got my cuffs on him. Better leave them there."

He studied Gilman with cold, flat eyes. "I'm expecting you to get him there alive, Rue."

Gilman's thick lips cracked into a grin. "I'll get him there, Sheriff. The being alive's going to be up to him."

Cole nodded to Shay. "You hear that? It's up to you. Behave yourself and you'll have no trouble. Try pulling something and I'll not take the responsibility for how it turns out."

"Seems to me," Jim replied indifferently, "nobody around here's very long on responsibility when it comes to doing right by a man."

George Cole grunted. He turned to Gilman. "Wait'll I get up front," he said. "Then move out. Got to keep that bunch talking."

Gilman watched until Cole was again framed in the jail's entrance; then, gripping Shay's arm, he pushed him toward the rear door. As Jim jerked away, the big deputy looked over his shoulder at Sierra and winked broadly.

"See you in church, *compadre*."

"*Adiós*," the Mexican replied, his dark face set in serious lines.

4

Within the sound of George Cole's voice still haranguing the crowd, Rue Gilman opened the rear door and stepped out. He stood in the blistering rays of the sun, glancing up and down the alley. Satisfied, he beckoned peremptorily to Shay.

"Come on, come on, goddam it."

Jim moved into the narrow passageway. The old lawman's voice came over the roof of the low building now rather than through it.

"This way," Gilman said. "Got the horses waiting in that old barn, straight ahead."

"Should have shucked those spurs," Jim observed, glancing down at the huge Spanish rowels strapped to Gilman's expensive, hand-tooled boots. "You're making one hell of a racket."

"I'll do the worrying about it," the deputy snapped.

They gained the abandoned barn and ducked through a side opening. Two horses were tethered to the sagging divider of the stalls. Jim felt a lift of pleasure run through him. Gilman had brought him his own horse, a long-legged black gelding he had bought up in Wyoming little more than a year ago. The gelding, recognizing him, whinnied softly at his approach. Shay rubbed his nose affectionately, wondering at the deputy's thoughtfulness; there would be some reason for it.

25

"Climb on him," Gilman grumbled. "Got no time to waste playing with that nag."

Shay pulled the leathers free, and awkwardly because of his linked wrists, mounted the saddle. He squared himself and faced Gilman, who stared at him intently.

"Better we get something straight, jailbird," the deputy said, leaning forward. "Was it my doing, I'd stand by and let them Vengadors have you—"

"I'll bet you would," Jim said dryly. "Still wouldn't wipe the blame for me being here off your hands. No matter what, you'd still remember it was your lying tongue that—"

"Me—hell!" Gilman snapped. "You put yourself where you are. Don't go blaming me for it—but I ain't got time to argue with you. Just telling you now, I'll blow your damn head off if you cross me. Nobody'd fault me if I did, either, feeling the way they do about you."

Shay fought to keep his temper down. "If you try, Gilman, better be sure you shoot straight. You'll never get a second chance."

"I never miss," the deputy said softly. "Now, line out. Head straight across the yard to that patch of apple trees, then cut right. We keep going that way until we reach Sandoval's wood yard, and from there it's due west."

Gilman paused, waited for comment from Shay. It did not come. He continued. "I'll be riding alongside you, making it look like a couple of people going somewheres. But I'll be setting with my hand on my gun, just waiting for you to make the wrong move. You get me?"

Jim remained silent. He wheeled the black about and started across the yard. He heard Rue Gilman blurt an oath and spin his horse about angrily.

"Damn you—I asked you a question—" he raged, coming up abreast in a sudden rush; his words trailed off as they rode.

Jim Shay was paying the lawman no attention. He was now as interested as the deputy in getting safely away from Sacramento Springs. Somewhere along the trail to Santa Fe he'd find his opportunity to jump Gilman and make an escape; how and when he had no idea. It was simply a matter of patience.

Then he would begin a search that would last until he found the old man and his mule team. He would be around somewhere, probably east of the Rio Grande, beyond the Jornada. Likely he had a ranch in the Arena Blanca country, or it could be farther on than that area of glistening white sand, in the hills behind the towering Capitans. That the old man was not settled in the Rio Grande Valley was apparent since no one had recognized his description—or perhaps no one wanted to.

Jim had been able to provide a good account of the man. Squat, yellow-bearded, well up in his sixties, he had pulled into the Slausson yard that Sunday morning almost at the same moment as Shay had. Jim had been the first to enter the house and find the bodies of the homesteader and his wife. He had stepped to the door and motioned for the older man to come and look.

The bearded man had entered, glanced around the ransacked, littered rooms, and then stood for a time studying the lifeless bodies.

"Weren't 'Paches," he had said. "Been some torturin' goin' on, but not the way they'd of done it. And the woman. 'Paches would have done fierce things to her. Was I guessin', I'd say outlaws—maybe Mexicans. And they was lookin' mighty hard for somethin' they wanted powerful bad. Spent a lot of time tryin' to make them poor folks talk, tell where it was."

Jim had agreed; the scene had struck him the same way. The old man had turned and shambled back to his light rig. "You're headin' north," he had said as he climbed back onto the seat of his creaking vehicle. "When you get to the Springs, tell the law. I got to be movin' right along."

Jim had watched him drive off, striking east toward the Rio Grande and the Jornada beyond. Then he had returned to the house, cut down the body of the slain man from where it hung suspended by the thumbs from the parlor ceiling, and placed it on the bed. The woman, her face a shapeless, lumpy mass from countless blows, lay on the floor. He had put her beside her husband.

He had just started for his horse when he heard a rider coming in from the north, and thinking it might be the killer returning, he had drawn his pistol and stepped back into the house. Watching the yard, he saw the rider enter. Sunlight glinted on the star he wore on his vest, and Jim had heaved a sigh of relief. Now he could turn the whole thing over to the law and be on his way.

But the lawman had been Rue Gilman, and he had drawn his own conclusions as to what had taken place in the Slausson home. . . .

"You won't be needing that gelding where you're going," Gilman said now, breaking into his thoughts. The deputy's voice was friendly. "Be real happy to take him off your hands."

Shay knew now why Gilman had brought the black. He gave the man's gross, sweaty face a disinterested glance, and said nothing. By now they were well away from the settlement, heading into a barren gray country that lay shimmering in the heat haze. Cholla cactus, mesquite, and sickly green creosote bush stood out starkly on the ragged land; they seemed to be wilting under the driving sun.

They had passed the dark ledges and narrow canyons of the Socorro Mountains, with their smooth, knobbed peaks, and the higher ridges of the Gallinas were beginning to show up to the north and west. Off to the right the faint smoke trails of Socorro could be seen against the burnished sky, and beyond it the white alkali streaks of the Rio Grande's dry bed.

"You hear me?" Gilman demanded, mopping at his florid face. "Said I'd—"

"I heard you," Shay said.

"What're you figuring to do with him?" the deputy persisted. "Can't just turn him loose. Now, you'd sure feel easier was you knowing somebody like me was looking after him, wouldn't you?"

"Forget it," Jim said. "I'm not done with him yet."

Gilman snorted and sat back on his saddle. "Maybe that's what you're thinking. You're wrong."

The afternoon wore on, blistering hot and dusty. A low bank of dirty clouds had piled up on the northern horizon, but overhead the sky was clear and there was no relief from the piercing heat. The endless stretches of glittering sand lay lifeless, and several times Rue Gilman swore deeply, angry at being compelled to pursue such a route. He loudly damned Shay for being the cause of it, George Cole for thinking of it—and the Vengadors for not grabbing their victim when they had the chance and making it easier for all. And he cursed himself for becoming a lawman in the first place.

Shay listened in silence to the deputy's mouthings, and longed for darkness to come. Not only would it bring surcease from the searing heat, but it might present the opportunity to escape. Then he would be free to double back and strike out eastward in his quest.

"Man needs a little money in the pen," Gilman said, picking up the refrain again. "Got to have tobacco and a bottle now and then. And I hear tell greasing the right palms will get a man a cute little *puta* for the night. All takes cash, howsomever."

Gilman paused, waited for his words to have effect. Jim, half listening, head down, his chin sunk into his chest, rode on silently.

"Was I to fork over, say twenty dollars for the black. You could keep your gear, sell it. That'd give you—"

"Oh, go to hell, Gilman!" Jim exclaimed, suddenly exasperated and dead weary of the talk. "Only way you'll ever get my horse is when I'm dead—and I don't plan on that very soon. Now, shut up and forget it."

The sham of friendliness dropped from Rue Gilman's manner. He brushed angrily at the sweat clouding his eyes. "Just might arrange that for you," he said quietly.

Jim didn't bother to answer. He looked ahead, his eyes squinting to cut down the glare. The jagged peaks of the Ladrones were becoming more articulate. He shifted his gaze toward the sun. They should reach the mountains around dark, he guessed; he settled back to sweat out the remainder of the journey.

Night had closed in completely when they gained the foothills at the base of the steep, brush-studded slopes and pulled to a halt beside a stand of junipers. Jim stayed on the black.

"Horses need water. Be smart to keep going until we find a spring."

"All dry canyons along here," Gilman said sourly, rising in his stirrups and looking around. "Have to water them from the canteens. By God, my butt feels like—"

Jim glanced up. The deputy was staring off into the night; something interested him. Shay raised himself to look.

The faint orange glow of a small cook fire filled a wash a

hundred yards or so ahead. Two figures hunched beside it. Gilman studied the pair, his moonlike face shadowed and still.

"Something plenty familiar about them jaspers," he said finally. "Expect I'd better have a look-see." He settled back on his saddle and glared at Shay. "Now, you do what I tell you or I'll be forking that black a lot sooner'n you think. Hear?"

Jim nodded. The two men at the fire could provide the opportunity he needed. He would play it meek, do just as Gilman ordered—and watch his chances.

"We'll ease in close so's I can make out who they are. You keep alongside me. And don't try nothing."

Shay lifted his arms slightly. "How the hell you think I can do anything with these on?" he said, exhibiting his manacled wrists.

"Wouldn't be knowing. I'm just telling you straight—try something smart and I'll blast you out of that saddle."

They moved forward, walking their horses slowly across the sand to deaden the sound of their approach. When they were within twenty yards Gilman lifted his broad hand. He peered through the brush, then swore softly and happily.

"Aaron Sanford and Dave Lund—sure as God made little toad frog! I'm sure running in luck," he added, glancing at Jim. "Nice fat rewards for both them boys. Wanted for sticking up a couple of stagecoaches. Get down real quiet now."

Shay dismounted and waited while Gilman tied the horses in a clump of low trees. Somewhere off in the hushed night an owl hooted a question.

"You want to give me a hand?" the deputy asked, reaching down and removing his spurs.

Jim shook his head. "Your fish. You fry them."

Gilman glared at him. "Ain't so sure about you, bucko! Maybe I ought to lay a gun barrel across your skull, keep you quiet for a spell."

"Don't try it," Shay said coolly, "unless you want me to yell. I do that and your birds will fly the coop fast. I'll give you no trouble—I'm just not mixing up in it."

Gilman considered that for a few moments. Apparently satisfied, he said, "Come on. Let's work in close."

5

Jim Shay moved forward. This could be the break he needed —but it could mean sudden death unless he used care, worked it right. He still wore the handcuffs, and the big deputy was right behind him, both guns ready. He twisted his head, glanced over his shoulder.

Gilman stared at him suspiciously, and motioned for him to go on. Shay continued picking his way quietly over the soft sand, slipping in among the clumps of saltbush and mesquite and the low mounds of rock washed down from higher levels during the infrequent storms that visited the desert.

The voices of the outlaws grew more distinct. Jim could see them fairly clearly through the sparse underbrush. Lund was an average-looking man, somewhere in his thirties. He had a lean, sardonic face with close-set eyes. Aaron Sanford was older, with that quiet, stilled manner of a killer about him. He was thin and tall; when he spoke he had a way of dropping his head and looking up through his brows.

"We'll find him, come daylight," he said.

"Dead man ain't no good to nobody," Lund answered in a dissatisfied voice. "Wish to hell you hadn't been so goddam handy with that hogleg of yours."

Sanford stirred down the froth in a lard can of coffee he had just removed from the fire. "He ain't dead . . . . Leastwise he wasn't last look I got of him."

"Could be by morning. We ought to keep hunting him."

31

Sanford scanned the rough slope rising before him impatiently. "You want to go stumbling around there, maybe break a leg, go right ahead. Me—I'm waiting for daylight."

Shay felt the muzzle of a pistol dig into his ribs. He stopped. They had reached the last fringe of brush at the edge of the firelight's fan. Gilman motioned for him to remain where he now crouched.

Shay moved his head up and down, signifying understanding. What the deputy's plan was he had no idea. Taking on two dangerous outlaws while encumbered with a prisoner who had avowed intentions to escape would require cleverness and efficiency, and he doubted if Rue Gilman possessed such qualities. But the lawman had nerve, he had to admit . . . nerve actuated by greed.

"God—I wish I had a drink," Dave Lund exclaimed suddenly. "Give a half interest in hell for a quart of old Jim Beam's bourbon right now!" He tossed the remainder of coffee in his cup onto the ground. "This hogwash—"

Rue Gilman rose to his towering height. In the flickering firelight he was a massive, shadow-wrapped shape.

"Hell to be dry, ain't it, Dave?"

Lund whirled, his jaw sagging. Aaron Sanford was up in a swift blur of motion, like the uncoiling of a steel spring. His hand lowered, then halted as his eyes came to rest on the twin muzzles of Gilman's cocked pistols.

"Now, just stand easy," the deputy drawled. "And start reaching. . . . High. . . . Sure is nice to find you boys here."

Lund, his first shock of surprise subsiding, said, "How'd you know about it?"

"Didn't. Just happened along," Gilman replied. Without looking down, he said, "Get up, jailbird. Walk out there by the fire so's I can watch you. Don't you get close to my prize babies."

The outlaws stared as Jim rose and moved into view. Lund said, "Who's he?"

"Little chore I'm doing . . . taking him to Santa Fe."

Shay halted several paces from the outlaws and turned.

"Reckon you'd better be getting rid of that hardware," the deputy said. "Dave, reach down with your left hand, pull your gun, and let it fall. You, too, Sanford. Now, do it sort of slow and easy. Been a long, hot day, and I'm kind of twitchy."

The outlaws complied with great care. It was clear Gilman was no stranger to them. Then the lawman said, "Just step back a mite."

The only sounds in the clearing were the popping of dry wood in the fire and the dry scuffing as Lund and Sanford backed away from their weapons.

"Turn around," Gilman ordered. "Keep your hands up high."

"What're you aiming to do?" Lund demanded.

"Well, I got me a little problem," Gilman said in a pseudo-confidential way. "Sure can't miss out on a couple of fat prizes like you two. But I still got to get this here prisoner of mine to the pen. Reckon I'm just going to have to stake you boys out until I can come back. . . ."

"Stake us out!" Lund echoed.

"Sure. Won't hurt you none. I'll be back in a couple of days." Gilman paused, his eyes on Sanford. "You ain't doing much talking, Aaron. What's the matter? You don't like what I'm saying?"

Sanford spat. "What's to talk about? You're holding the iron."

"That's being real smart. I got five slugs in each one of these forty-fives . . . five for each of you. Keep thinking about that while you're looking the other way."

Gilman quietly holstered one of his weapons and stepped forward. He kicked away the pistols Lund and Sanford had dropped into the brush, then beckoned to Shay.

"I'll be needing them cuffs you're wearing," he said in a low voice. He produced the key Cole had given him. "Got another pair in my pocket, but I'll have to use them, too. You letting me take them off without any trouble—or had I best rap you good a couple of times?"

"Take them off," Jim said. He held out his arms.

Again the deputy studied him closely. He nodded. "Keep playing it smart and we'll get along," he said, and removed the manacles. He reached into his pocket for a second pair.

"Get back over there where you were. Makes it easy to keep an eye on you."

Jim Shay, his nerves pulling taut, backed slowly to his place near the dwindling fire. Gilman watched narrowly.

"Fine, fine," he said. "Don't move a toe. Just keep thinking how easy it'd be for me to cut you down, was you to start running."

Shay returned the deputy's stare coldly. Gilman, with his three prisoners lined up before him, had them dead to rights. He could make short work of any—or all—if they attempted to make a break. The lawman manipulated the handcuffs, opening the notched jaws wider. Then he glanced around. A squat juniper with a twisted, fair-sized trunk stood at his right.

"Ought to be just the ticket," he said. "They sure won't be pulling it loose." He hunched down by the tree, fastened one of the cuffs to the trunk, and closed it tight. Then he affixed the second pair of manacles slightly above the first. Testing them, and finding them secure, he drew back.

"You boys ought to be thanking me," he said. "You'll be laying in the shade while I'm gone."

Without daring to turn, Lund said, "Sure, sure, we're thanking you—for nothing."

"Why, I figured you'd be right pleased," Gilman said. "Could've planted you out in the sun. Ought to be glad I got a kind heart."

Jim Shay waited and listened. He was in a bad position to attempt anything; he faced Gilman, and his slightest move would draw the deputy's instant attention.

It was a long ten yards to the first clump of brush on the slope and the darkness beyond it. He wondered how fast Rue Gilman really was; big men usually moved slow . . . If he could get the jump on him—he just might make it. . . .

"You're first, Dave," Gilman said, still in a jocular mood. "Time for bed. Come here and let me tuck you in."

Lund wheeled slowly. His glance came to rest on the juniper. "You mean you're handcuffing us to that tree—leaving us here while you go clear to Santa Fe and back?"

"Sure enough, that's what I'm doing. Like I told you, it ought to be right comfortable there in the shade while I'm gone." His tone shifted abruptly. "Come on, come on! I ain't got the whole night."

Lund shuffled toward the juniper. Keeping his gun up, his eyes switching constantly from Lund to Sanford to Shay and back again, the deputy waited. When Lund had squatted down, Gilman said, "Put that cuff on—and be damn sure it's clamped tight. I'll be looking it over, so don't try fooling me."

The outlaw fitted the steel circle to his wrist. It snapped loudly as it ratcheted into place.

"Now you, Mr. Sanford," Gilman said. "It's your turn to climb in bed—"

"The hell it is, you fat bastard!" Sanford yelled, and spun around.

As he turned, his shape an indistinct blur, he folded forward. Fire spat from his hand as he squeezed off a shot from a small weapon he had concealed.

Breath gushed from Rue Gilman's lips as a bullet drove into him. Sanford triggered a second shot. The force of it wrenched an agonized cry from the deputy's flaring mouth. He stumbled forward, went to his knees.

Jim Shay whirled and raced for the safety of the slope.

Running recklessly, Shay reached the shadows, threw himself behind a clump of yellow-flowered rabbit brush, and crawled hurriedly on until he was in the deep pool of darkness beneath a large rock. He lay there, breathing heavily. A yell went up from the clearing.

"That jasper Gilman had with him—he's getting away. Head him off!"

That was Lund's voice. Immediately Sanford answered. "Got to have a gun . . . Derringer's empty!"

"Use the deputy's . . . ."

Shay drew himself to his feet. Crouching, he rushed on into the night, losing himself in the rocks and scanty brush that littered the rough, wild terrain.

"He's gone . . . . Ain't no use trying to catch him now." It was Lund again. His voice now was faint, receding. "Get the key off the deputy. Turn me loose."

Shay halted again, and leaned against a smooth-shouldered ledge. He was sucking deep for wind, and the muscles of his legs ached from the strain of running uphill. He listened into the darkness, trying to catch more of what was being said by the outlaws. They were far below. All he could hear was a low mumble.

He wondered if they would come after him. They had known he was Gilman's prisoner, and from that would conclude he was an outlaw. It placed them on common ground, so possibly they would forget him. That would suit him fine;

he could double back to the gelding, mount up, and be on his way.

A rock rattled on the slope below. Shay came upright, his senses tingling. He heard Aaron Sanford swear in a hard, dry voice. From a short distance to the outlaw's right, Lund called out, "Spot him?"

"No," Sanford grumbled. "Wasn't nothing. . . ."

"Going to be hell running him down in the dark. Like the other one. Maybe he'll keep his mouth shut. Probably had no use for Gilman, either."

"Ain't taking no chances," Sanford said. "Being wanted for holdup and wanted for killing a lawman's two different things. I aim to make damn sure he don't do no talking. Keep moving, he ain't gone far."

"Seems I recollect you wasn't so keen about climbing around on this damn hill a while back," Lund observed. "Wanted to wait for sunup."

"This is different," Sanford replied.

Shay turned and started on. He made his way carefully now, trying to make no sound. He continued climbing, working his way toward a jagged peak. The grade was steep and rough, and he was grateful for the occasional junipers and lesser brush and the mounds of rocks that not only afforded support but also provided protection from the moon, steadily rising now.

He hoped Sanford and Lund wouldn't think of the horses. They would have him cold if they did. All they had to do was drop back and wait somewhere close by the gelding, knowing that eventually he would try to reach it. In this country a man went nowhere without a horse.

Jim began to search his mind for a plan to reach the gelding before the outlaws stumbled on the same idea. He was about two-thirds of the way up the slope. The horses were now behind him and to the south of the mountain, which was gradually becoming more barren.

He listened intently. For a full minute there was only the far-off yelping of a coyote, and then he heard the dry snap of a stick. The outlaws were directly below him, coming straight upgrade. Likely they would be only a short distance apart. They had heard him moving, just as he had detected them. No matter how careful a man might be, it

was impossible not to create a certain amount of noise crossing the loose rock and moving through the sun-dried brush.

Shay mopped at the sweat on his forehead. Despite the
cool breeze drifting in from the southwest, he was soaking
wet. He waited on the slope, crouched in the darkness. They
could follow him simply by listening. By listening—maybe
he could sucker them off onto the north side of the mountain
by drawing their attention to that point, then double back
to the horses.

He moved on, still using care. They would hear him anyway, thanks to the dry brush and the slanting beds of loose
gravel and shale.

He worked his way transversely across the slope, holding
the high peak to his left. The moon was out full strength now,
and the areas outside the clusters of scrubby growth and rock
were flooded with soft silver light. He avoided those islands
meticulously.

With the peak finally well behind his left shoulder, Jim
stopped and again listened into the silence. Once more he
heard the sound of the doggedly pursuing outlaws. This
time the noise, a faint rattle of pebbles, appeared to be nearer.

He picked up a stone. This had better work, he told himself
grimly. Unless he could get Sanford and Lund off his heels he
was done for. He threw the stone off into the night. It
struck far down on the north slope, rattled noisily, started
a small cascade of lesser-sized gravel. Instantly Lund's hoarse
whisper cracked the stillness.

"Hear that?"

"I heard," Sanford's low, controlled voice replied. "He's
heading down the hill."

Immediately Jim heard a branch snap, and then the
sound of rocks being displaced, spilling off onto the grade,
as the two men started angling for the base of the north
slope at a hurried pace. He breathed deeper.

He resisted the urge to turn and hurry for the opposite side
of the mountain. No point in creating a racket now that
might bring the outlaws back. Give them time to reach the
foot of the slope first.

He waited until he could no longer hear them, and then,
wheeling, began to slice across the hillside. If he followed a
direct line he could save considerable time and distance. The

horses were tethered opposite his present location, and below. Cutting across instead of dropping to the level of the mesa and then moving southward would eliminate circling the mountain at its base.

He hurried on, still careful to be fairly quiet, confident the outlaws would be unable to detect the subdued sounds of his passage. The coyote had been joined by several of his kin, and their discordant barking seemed nearer. That was reassuring.

Again breathless, he paused to get his bearings. He was dead in line with the peak, still two-thirds of the way up. The going would be easier from there on. He could begin slanting downgrade. He studied the blurred land below, tried to figure exactly where Gilman had left the horses. In that patch of junipers beyond the first high mound of rocks, he thought. But he ought to be sure. He would have no time to waste searching about in the night. Sanford and Lund would realize they had been fooled soon, and start back. He should—

Shay came to sudden attention. A strong current of alarm raced through him. His ears had picked up a sound—a human sound. It was close by. Motionless, scarcely breathing, he hung there, a crouched shape in the silver shine of the night.

He heard the noise again. A low moan. He came about slowly, eyes on a brushy bench immediately to his right. It fronted a hollowed-out cove on the face of the slope. He studied it for several moments, then crept forward silently. Reaching the line of tangled growth, he looked behind it.

The black, rectangular entrance to a mine met his glance. Half in, half out of this lay a man.

7

Jim dropped to his knees and crawled in behind the brow of saltbush and thorny briar. He leaned over the still figure.

The man was young, somewhere in his twenties, dressed in the rough clothing of a prospector. Blood soaked the front of his coarse, linsey-woolsey shirt, and in the pale light of the moon his whiskered face had a glazed, bluish color. Shay placed his fingers over the man's heart and felt for a beat. It was there, slow and labored.

At the pressure of Jim's fingers, the prospector's eyes fluttered and opened. Immediately they filled with alarm. This would be the man the outlaws had spoken of, the one they had been hunting.

"It's all right," Jim said. "I'm a friend."

"Friend? You ain't one of them?"

"No. . . . Fact is I'm on the dodge from them, too."

Shay looked into the mine-shaft opening. It had been enlarged and shaped into a circular room. He could see mining tools, boxes that contained supplies, and other articles stacked along the rough walls. A pallet, unrolled, lay near the center. Evidently it was the prospector's living quarters.

"I'll get you inside," he said. "See if I can stop the bleeding. Who are you?"

"Name's Garrick," the wounded man said. "No use patching me up. Bullet went clean through, tore me up something fierce. Reckon I'm done for."

Shay took Garrick by the shoulders, and gently as possible,

40

moved him onto the pallet. He wished he might light the lantern hanging from its peg on the wall, but he dared not; a square of lamplight on the slope of the mountain would serve as a beacon to Lund and Sanford.

He pulled back the blood-soaked shirt, examining the wound as best he could by the filtered moonlight. The prospector was right. It was a matter of time. Jim sat back. Taking up a strip of cloth, he fashioned a pad, placed it against the opening left by the bullet, and made Garrick as comfortable as possible.

"Obliged to you—"

"Shay . . . Jim Shay."

"Shay. Glad I won't end up laying out there. Plenty of coyotes on the mountain. And buzzards."

Jim cast a glance at the entrance to the cave. He was losing precious moments; he should be getting off the mountain. Sanford and Lund would have discovered their error by now. "Don't figure I got long," Garrick said in a low voice. "There's —there's a favor I want to ask."

Jim said, "Sure. What's this all about? How come they're after you?"

"Gold," Garrick said. "They're looking for my gold."

Shay stared. "You found gold—here in the Ladrones?"

"A little. They had in mind I had a big poke, was trying to make me tell where it's hid. Slipped away from them. . . . Got shot doing it. . . . So I crawled here . . . most of the way Reckon I lost them. . . ."

"They were going to start hunting for you in the morning. Knew you'd been hit. I heard them talking about it."

"All a big laugh—big mistake. There ain't no gold. . . . Sure a joke on me . . . getting killed for some gold I don't even have. . . ."

Shay frowned. "Kind of a tough joke. Where'd they get the idea in the first place?"

"Hard telling. You know how tales get started. . . . Rumors and such. . . . Could've been some of my doings. . . . Brings me to that favor I mentioned."

Jim stirred. "Do what I can for you, Garrick. I'm in sort of a jam myself."

"Won't cost you nothing. . . . And it won't take no lot of

time. All mighty heavy on my mind, and I want to set things straight before—before I kick off."

Shay studied the prospector's tormented face. The man was steadily growing weaker. Abruptly Jim pushed his own pressing needs aside; he could hear the dying man out, at least, and do what he might to ease his conscience.

"You give me your word, Shay?"

"You've got it."

"Good. . . . Real obliged. . . . Wouldn't feel right dying, leaving Stella there . . . waiting. . . ."

"Stella?"

"Girl I know . . . figured to marry. Lives in Sacramento Springs. . . . Maybe you've seen her. Works sometimes in a saloon . . . one they call the Mexican Hat. . . ."

Shay shook his head. "Afraid not. Sort of a stranger around there."

"Prettiest bit of fluff you ever saw. We been running together about a year. . . . Figured to marry up soon as I got me a big stake. Then we was pulling out . . . heading for San Francisco. . . . Stella always wanted to live in San Francisco."

Garrick began to cough. His body shook from the effort, and when the spasm was over he lay back limp, his eyes closed.

"This favor—you want me to tell her, Stella, what happened? That it?" Shay asked gently.

Garrick's lids pulled back. "Part of it. . . . See, it was this here way. Stella could have had her pick of a lot of men. . . . She took up with me instead. Seen her in the Mexican Hat one day. Had me a little poke of nuggets I'd scrounged off'n the mountain. She come over and we got to talking. . . . Was real pleased to know me, she said. . . ."

The poor devil. . . . This Stella had been interested in his gold nuggets, not him, Shay thought uncomfortably. Garrick should have had sense enough to realize that.

"We got to seeing each other regular after that. . . . I'd drop by her place whenever I'd hit town. About once a month. One day we got to talking marriage, and I asked her about hitching up . . . with me. She told me flat out she was crazy enough about me and she'd do it in a minute . . . only she'd made up her mind a long time ago she wasn't marrying no man who didn't have money . . . plenty of

money. . . . Said she wanted to quit working in a saloon. . . .
Wanted it fixed so's she'd never have to see the inside of one
again. . . . What she wanted was a home . . . kids. . . ."

Again Garrick's voice faltered, and he went into a series
of deep, wrenching coughs that brought flecks of blood to
his lips. Then he lay quiet, breathing hoarsely in quick, short
gasps.

"Better forget talking," Jim said. "Just rest."

"Nope . . . got to get this said. . . . Be fine in a couple of
minutes. . . ."

A couple of minutes could cost me my life, Shay thought,
and the urge to leave the mine shaft, stuffy with the past
day's heat, the smell of death, pressed harder upon him.

"Right there's where I made my . . . mistake. . . ,"
Garrick muttered. "Started laying it on thick to Stella.
Wanted her so bad I told her . . . I had plenty of money. . . .
Said I'd struck color and it was paying big. Know I shouldn't
have lied, but it was plain it was the only way . . . the only
way I could hold her. . . . Make her think I had a lot
of gold salted away. . . .

"When she heard that she really showed . . . how much I
meant to her. Couldn't do enough for me. Was making big
plans all the time. I made her promise to keep quiet about
it. Said I didn't want no gold rush started up here in . . . in the
Ladrones. She offered to keep my stake I said I was building,
but I told her I'd already made arrangements. Was sending
it to my sister who was putting it back for me until I come
for it. . . . Made a real brag about how much gold I had saved
up. Told her it was nigh on to thirty thousand dollars worth.

"She was willing to head for San Francisco right then.
Said we'd have plenty. That sort of threw me. But I got around
it by telling her . . . I'd set my sights on fifty thousand dollars
. . . and nothing was going to stop me until I got that much.

"So I managed to hang onto her while . . . all the time I
kept looking for color, hoping I'd strike it rich and could
quit my lying to her. Can see now I was wrong. But was the
only way I could hold her . . . keep her wanting to marry me.
She'd of dropped me quick, was she to know the truth. . . .
And maybe she'd of kept on loving me, like she said, but she'd
of likely ended up marrying somebody else . . . because he
had big money. I sure couldn't . . . have stood that."

"Must be quite a woman," Shay said.

"She sure is. . . . You'll find that out when you see her. . . ."

"Been thinking about that. You said she lived in the Springs. Right now that's not a very healthy place for me. There's been some trouble—"

Garrick lifted his head suddenly. Worry filled his eyes. "Won't take you but a few minutes. She lives all by herself . . . house out at the edge of town. On the road to Magdalena. You'll find it easy. . . . Little dobe place . . . doors painted red. Shay—you promised . . . gave your word. . . ."

Jim sighed quietly. Sweat was beading his forehead again from the relentless pressure. Somewhere outside, undoubtedly near by now, were Aaron Sanford and Dave Lund. They would still be searching for him—or they could have thought of the horses and be down there in ambush, waiting for him.

And now—even if his luck held and he managed to escape them, he had jockeyed himself into returning to Sacramento Springs and carrying out a promise he'd made impulsively to a dying man. What the hell was getting into him? He must be going softheaded. Frustration and impatience edged his voice when he spoke.

"All right. What do I tell this Stella?"

"Truth," Garrick murmured, relieved. In the pale light stealing through the opening to the shaft, the harsh lines in his face disappeared and a sort of repose settled over him.

"The plain truth. Want her to know how it was with me. Tell her there wasn't any gold . . . never was. But I was working hard to find some for her. God knows I worked . . . like a dog. But I never could have no luck. . . .

"I done wrong . . . telling her lies. But this ought to set things straight for her. Sure wouldn't want her waiting around . . . maybe missing her chance. Ain't right she should keep waiting . . . for me. . . ."

Jim Shay's temper softened. The poor blind fool. Stella wouldn't be just waiting around. She didn't sound like the kind. She would be making her way in every way possible, hoping perhaps this big, ungainly man would show up one day with a bag of gold. And she would undergo no heartbreak when she learned of his death.

"Shay . . . you'll sure see her, tell her?"

Jim nodded. "First thing in the morning."

The repose deepened on Garrick's sallow features. He closed his eyes, smiled vaguely as his breath began to come and go in brief, shallow rasps. He had expended what little strength he had.

"Sure . . . feel better," he muttered. "Mighty glad you come along . . . Shay. Wouldn't want Stella wasting her life . . . waiting . . . for me . . . not knowing. . . ." He raised his head suddenly again in an unexpected show of strength. His voice was shrill. "You . . . you'll sure see her? You ain't just telling me you will?"

"I'll see her," Shay said, pressing the man back onto the blankets.

He would be endangering himself and further delaying the search for the old man and the mules, but he would go through with it. He had said he would.

"I'll tell her the whole story—right from the start—"

Jim stopped. He looked closely at Garrick. He was speaking to a dead man.

8

Garrick would worry no more about his Stella—whoever she might be. He was out of it, finished with the sorrows, the brutal pressures, the fears, the labors that all men face while they live. It was just as well he would never know his Stella was likely not worth the price he had paid.

Jim Shay leaned forward, unbuckled the gun belt Garrick wore, and lifting the dead man slightly, drew it from him. Placing it about his own waist, he drew the gun and examined it. It was an old Colts Dragoon, cap and ball, forty-four with a Thuer conversion to cartridges. The action was gritty, but it was in fair condition. There were five shells in the cylinder, a dozen more scattered through the loops in the belt.

Shay thrust his hand into the man's pockets. He took a jackknife from one, some loose change, amounting to three dollars or so, from the other.

Then he picked up a dusty blanket from the hard-packed dirt floor and covered the prospector. He would tell Stella where Garrick lay, and she could send someone for the body.

He moved to the mouth of the shaft. A makeshift door of scrap lumber hung from leather hinges. Listening first, and hearing nothing, he bent low and stepped out into the narrow cleared space behind the wall of brush. He pulled the door shut and jammed it tight. Dropping to his knees, he crawled back onto the slope.

There he paused again to listen and scan the silvered hillside. Nothing. He moved on downgrade, disturbed because

46

he could not locate Sanford and Lund, yet hopeful that he would not. Perhaps they had given up searching for him on the mountain, and were lying in ambush near the horses. If so, he had a weapon of his own now, and if they wanted to make a shoot-out of it, he could accommodate them.

The moon was at full strength, and the world about him was flooded with light. The coyote chorus had increased its membership and was setting up an infernal racket in the direction of the dry-bedded Rio Salado.

He went on. He raked his hand against a cholla in his haste, cursed softly at the stinging pain. Pausing, he listened again into the warm hush. Off to his right now there was a faint scraping, but it was only some small animal—a kangaroo rat or possibly a nocturnal ground squirrel. He moved on. He could not afford the luxury of wasted time; he must be far from Sacramento Springs by daylight, into country where his chances of stumbling on someone who would recognize him would be remote.

But first he had to go to Sacramento Springs.

He cursed himself again for being a softhearted fool and allowing himself to be dragged into such a situation. He had been loco to promise Garrick he'd look up his lousy, gold-crazy whore! What the hell was the matter with him, anyway? He could be putting himself right back on the road to the pen again!

But he'd promised Garrick. It actually wouldn't be much out of his way. He wanted to get on the far side of the town, anyway. That was where he had last seen the bearded man— at the Slausson place, which lay fifty miles or so south of the settlement.

He had intended to swing wide of the town, take no chances on being spotted. He could change the plan a bit, keep farther to the west. Fortunately Stella's house lay in that direction.

He pressed on quietly and hurriedly downslope toward the junipers where he figured the horses had been tethered. There were no signs of the outlaws, and the conviction grew within him that they were waiting somewhere near his black and the heavy-footed gray Rue Gilman had ridden. He could expect a fight. He rounded a shoulder of rock.

"Hey—who—"

At the startled question Jim Shay jerked to a halt. The dark shape of a man loomed up from the shadows, blocking the trail.

Shay had a momentary glimpse of Dave Lund's surprised features. He threw himself against the outlaw.

Lund tried to leap aside, but the rock had him trapped. The two men came together with jarring force. Breath exploded from the outlaw's lungs in a gusty blast as he slammed up against the granite surface. Shay lashed out savagely. His balled fist caught Lund somewhere on the face, driving his head against the boulder a second time.

He must silence the outlaw before he could yell to Aaron Sanford. Jim hammered a hard left to Lund's belly, and then a final right to his jaw.

Lund sagged. Shay drove him to his knees, chopping him mercilessly about the head and shoulders. The outlaw wilted, and sprawled out full-length at the base of the rock.

Shay stepped back, straining to hear above the rasp of his own labored breathing. He could pick up no sounds. He hurried on down the slope. Either Sanford had not heard the disturbance or he had and was moving in stealthily. It would be smart to move away from Lund quickly.

Almost at the foot of the grade he once more stopped to listen. The coyotes had quieted, and now he heard only the faint clicking of insects in the rocks about him. He turned, looked up the steep slope; where the hell was Aaron Sanford?

He was farther over, Jim decided. That would have been the natural plan for them to make—one watch the south, the other the east. He could spare no more time speculating over it. Midnight was not far off, and he must be on the trail to Sacramento Springs.

He reached the foot of the slope and angled toward the scrubby growth where the horses had been tethered. It was a good two hundred yards distant, but there were ample brush and rock to mask his movements. He doubted if Sanford, looking down from the mountain, could see him. Dave Lund, however, would be regaining consciousness soon, and could be depended upon to start yelling.

He wound his way through the greasewood and grayish saltbush at a fast walk, instinctively making his passage as quiet as possible. He saw the horses then, standing where he had thought they would be. Only their heads were visible above the junipers. They were fifteen or twenty yards away. He began to run—then pulled up abruptly as a rank odor assailed his nostrils.

Tobacco smoke!

Shay froze, fearing to turn his head. So Sanford had come down alone to wait while Lund remained on the mountain.

He grinned into the night. Aaron Sanford had tipped his hand by indulging in a quirley. Jim raised a finger to his lips and wet it, testing the faint breeze. It was coming from the southwest. That meant the outlaw was below the horses.

Silently he doubled over his tracks and circled in considerably below the junipers where the horses were tied. He moved slowly through the brush, his eyes probing the shadows for the outlaw.

Then he saw the red, glowing tip as Sanford sucked deep on his cigarette; it faded as the outlaw exhaled. The man was less than a dozen paces away. He drew the old Colts, and quiet as spreading light, eased in.

He reached a point where Sanford was little more than an arm's length away. Jim lurched for the man's head.

Sanford whirled. The butt of the old Dragoon caught him a sharp blow near the temple. He dropped without a sound.

Shay hurried on to the black. He jerked the reins loose, and vaulted to the saddle. Spinning the big horse around, he struck off toward Sacramento Springs at a fast gallop.

The black jogged on tirelessly through the night, crossing the barren, rolling hills, the shallow ravines, the wide
expanse of finest gypsum known as the Shifting Sands. Jim,
feeling the weight of the sleepless hours, dozed on and off,
never for long.

Around three o'clock, with the sharp chill of dawn approach-
ing, he halted on the last high, purple-shadowed ridge north
of the settlement, and looked down on the collection of buildings. Separate squares of yellow light at opposite ends of the
main street marked the locations of the two all-night saloons.
Save for those soft-edged glows, Sacramento Springs lay
silent and dark.

He swung west from there, riding a rock-studded hogback
for a time, and finally dropped off into a well-tended field of
corn. Stella's house stood along the road to Magdalena,
Garrick had said; by angling across he should eventually
intercept that dusty trail.

A short time later he reached the outlying residences.
He began to thread the black through littered yards, passing
frequent evil-smelling privies, rousing numerous dogs into
frantic, noisy activity, and finally arrived at the well-traveled
road that connected the two settlements.

Garrick had not said how far from town Stella lived. She
could be to his left, nearer to the houses, or she might be
farther out on the way to Magdalena. He judged that she

probably lived a considerable distance from the Springs and accordingly swung right.

Minutes later he saw the house described by Garrick, a squat adobe with doors and window frames painted a garish red, hunched in the center of a neglected yard. A heat-shriveled tree, thinly leaved, struggled for life a short distance to one side; the well house, the sagging barn, and the privy all needed paint badly.

Shay drew abreast. A lone horse, hipshot and weary, stood at the hitchrack in the rear. Jim swore softly. Stella had company. Now more time would be lost. But he would have to wait.

He circled the house at a distance, and behind a crumbling adobe wall near the barn he dismounted, stretched his muscles, and squatted against the wall. Shortly after, the door to Stella's house opened and a man emerged. He walked at an unsteady gait to his mount, and climbed heavily onto the saddle. Jim watched him wheel out of the yard. Then he rose and walked quickly to the rear of the house. The door was locked, and he rapped lightly. There was no response. He knocked again. This time a feminine voice, drugged from sleeplessness, slowed by liquor, replied irritably.

"I'm tired. . . . Go someplace else."

The eastern sky beyond the Capitans showed a hint of dull gray. Impatient, Jim hammered at the flimsy panel.

"Let me in. It's important."

There was silence. Finally a key grated in the lock. The door opened a narrow crack. Jim booted it wide and stepped into the kitchen.

Stella, in a soiled wrapper that hung loosely about her body, a lamp in her hand, stared at him.

"Who the hell you think you are?"

"You're Stella, aren't you?"

"What if I am? Take your lousy money and go find somebody else."

"I'm not interested in you," Jim snapped. He pointed to a straight-backed chair. "Sit down and listen to me—and listen good. I've no time to chew it twice."

A deep anger came to her drawn features. She was still young, but a hard, tough woman who looked capable of almost anything. She placed the lamp on a table, and sank onto a chair. The house reeked of stale cigar smoke, musty bedding, and an oversweet perfume. Stifled by the rancid aura, Jim raised a window.

"What's so important?"

Stella was far from the beauty Garrick had pictured. In the light of the lamp on the table Jim could see that her eyes were small, deep-set and cunning. Her mouth was slack, pulled down at the corners, and her cheeks were lined and tended to hollowness. Patches of dried sweat crusted her neck, and her hair, hanging loosely about her shoulders, looked coarse and dull.

She was studying him, too. "I know you," she said abruptly. "You're that killer the deputy was taking to Santa Fe."

He brushed that aside. "I'm here about Garrick."

Stella leaned forward. Her eyes narrowed. "What about Cal Garrick?"

"He's dead. Found him in the Ladrones, a bullet through his chest. Died about a half hour after I ran across him."

Stella's mouth tightened with eagerness. "He give you something for—a letter or a message of some kind?"

"Wanted me to tell you he was dead so you wouldn't keep waiting for him. And that there wasn't any gold."

She came upright in a sudden movement. "No gold—that's a goddam lie! He told me—"

"I know what he told you." Shay repeated all that the prospector had said to him. Half crouched on the chair, Stella stared at him without moving until he had finished.

"It's a lie," she said finally, her voice flat. "I don't believe any of it."

Jim shrugged. "Suit yourself, but that's the way it is. You want to send for the body, you'll find—"

"To hell with the body!" she shouted with sudden violence. "You're trying to pull a ringer on me. I don't know what's going on—how you got away from Gilman—but I can guess. You killed him and started running. You saw Cal—killed him, too, and took his gold. That's what happened. You killed him—stole his gold."

Her words jarred Shay. He stiffened. The outlaws would probably leave the country, leave him holding the bag. He could expect to be credited with two more murders now.

"You're loco," he said wearily. "You think I'd come here—take all this trouble to tell you about Garrick, if I had?"

"You don't want somebody trailing you—that's why. You think by handing me this bunch of crap, I won't raise a fuss."

"Law's already looking for me, or soon will be. One more reason's not going to make a difference."

"There's a reason—just what I don't know yet, but I'll figure it out. And you're not getting away with it. I've been waiting a whole year for that gold. I don't aim to get cheated out of it now."

"You're not getting cheated—for the simple reason Garrick had no gold to start with. Best thing you can do is forget it."

"That gold belongs to me!" Stella screamed, lunging at Shay, clawing at his face. "You can't have it!"

Jim, white with anger, knocked her hands away and pushed her roughly into the chair. He wheeled toward the door.

"You've been told the truth," he said in a hard voice. "I did it as a favor to Garrick—a promise to a dying man. Now, believe what you please."

"You're damned right I will!" she screamed again. "And just as soon as I can get to town—"

Shay spun about, alarmed. He couldn't afford to let George Cole, or anyone else in Sacramento Springs, learn of his escape from Gilman until he was out of the country. As it stood, the day would likely pass before the fact became known—and then the sheriff would have no idea of the direction he had taken. Stella could change all that.

His mouth settled into a grim line. He crossed the room in quick strides. Seizing her by the arm, he jerked her to her feet and propelled her into the adjoining bedroom. She cursed him steadily, wildly, striking at him with her free hand. He warded off the blows, lifted her bodily, and threw her onto the bed.

"Stay there!" he growled. "Don't want to crack your head with my gun barrel, but I'll sure as hell do it if you keep this up."

"Your gun!" she shouted. "That's Cal's gun. I'd know it anywhere."

"Mine now," he snapped. He jerked a sheet off a chair and ripped it into strips. She cursed him steadily. But when he turned to her coldly she cringed.

"What're you doing?"

"Making sure you don't shoot off your mouth until I'm long gone." He bound her ankles with the lengths of soiled cloth. Then he tied her wrists and placed a gag over her mouth. She struggled fiercely, her hate-filled eyes never leaving him. He grinned as he stepped back to survey his work.

"Somebody'll be dropping by," he said. "Popular lady like you's bound to have visitors."

She thrashed about, raging something at him, but the words were smothered by the gag. Shay turned into the kitchen. He glanced through the smudged glass of the window. The gray to the east was turning into pale yellow, shot with soaring tentacles of lavender.

He let himself out and hurried to the waiting gelding.

10

He loped the gelding east toward Sacramento Springs for a short mile, then cut away, dropping off into a sandy, storm-washed gravel arroyo. He was in a desolate gray foothill area, an untamed strip that lay between the lush, cultivated valley adjacent to the river and the dark-sloped San Mateo Mountains to the west.

He did not like it. He was in the open. There were too many houses spaced along the edge of the valley, and the people in them were waking up. At the moment he was just a distant rider to them, moving south, and those noting his passage would give it only casual thought. Later, however, when Sheriff George Cole made inquiries as to a man on a black horse, they would recall seeing him.

It would be wiser to get back on the higher level of the mesa, near to the mountains. There would be no one along that flat, wind-scoured, sun-scorched surface. This meant going a good ten miles out of his way, but it was a worthwhile precaution.

Dawn caught him a short time later as he climbed from the last ravine and came out onto the prairie.

In the early light, Sacramento Springs had become a distant cluster of trees, upward-curling smoke, and soft-edged buildings. The steeple of a church lifted above all else, the cross rising from its steep triangle etched blackly against the brightening sky. Farther east, beyond the willows and cottonwoods, a narrow silver streak marked the trace of the

55

Rio Grande. It was low at this time of year, no more than fifty feet across at its widest and scarcely knee-deep to a fording horse.

Dry, white, baked sand extended from its crumbling edge toward the sun to merge eventually with that unreal, fierce wasteland known as the Jornada del Muerto—the Journey of Death. Beginning not far north of the Mexican border, the Jornada was a ninety-mile waterless hell. Ranging in width to as much as fifty miles, it lay as a merciless barrier to the east; swept by frequent sandstorms, shriveled and blistered by searing hundred-degree-plus heat in the daylight hours, scoured further at night by ceaseless winds that blew hot and cold, it was an exiled land.

Only a fool or a hard-pressed man would try to cross it while the sun rode the steel-blue heavens; few made the journey even by night. It was much better to take the long way around, to follow the trails above or below.

Once before Jim had approached this desolate, mysteriously beautiful, death-ridden vacuum. It had left him shaken, and he had vowed never to consider it again. But the old man had headed this way with his mules, evidently planning to travel during the darkness.

Shay put the gelding into motion; with the crescent chain of the San Mateos far to his right, he struck off at a comfortable jog. He had slept a bit during the night on the way back from the Ladrones, but he was beginning to feel the clawing of an empty stomach.

He had the money he had taken from Cal Garrick's pocket, but it was of little use to him now. Perhaps he could stop at one of the farms or ranches that lay much farther along in the valley.

He could not hope to remain unrecognized for long. Stella had brought that fact home to him forcefully. Now others would believe he had slain Rue Gilman during an escape. And he would be accused also of killing and robbing Garrick. All told, in fact, he now had four murders and a robbery chalked up against his name.

He grinned ruefully. How the hell could he prove he hadn't shot Gilman—or put a fatal bullet through Cal Garrick? There was a good chance he could clear himself of the Slaussons' murders, once he located the old man—but that wouldn't be enough now.

He could thank Dave Lund and Aaron Sanford for part of his troubles. Those lousy bastards, if they'd had the guts to stick around, were probably claiming that he had cut down the lawman. And Garrick—credit Stella for that. She believed that he had killed and robbed the young prospector. She would blat that all over town—and George Cole, in the light of other developments, would believe her.

Jim brushed at the sweat on his whiskered face. It was close to hopeless. A man with a lick of good sense would chuck the whole thing, keep right on going until he crossed the border to Mexico, only a couple of hundred miles ahead.

But Jim Shay disliked being pushed around. The thought of running and hiding, of never again being able to move about freely, galled him. Somehow he would prove he was innocent of all the charges now stacked up against him. Then he could go on living the free life he had always led. At the head of the list came the Slaussons' murders. And after clearing that up he could round up Dave Lund and Sanford; he would force them to tell the truth.

Now the sun had reached its zenith; it blazed into him. His hunger had increased. And there were no more than two or three swallows of water left in his canteen. He raised himself in his stirrups. Back across the shimmering layers of heat lay the blur that was Sacramento Springs. He should be far enough now from the settlement to risk scrounging a meal. . . . And he should begin making inquiries about the old man.

Suddenly riders broke into his vision. Two parties. The first, a group of five, perhaps six, were outlined briefly on a long running ridge south and west of the Springs. They moved toward him, small, indistinct dots, and then began to fall out of sight.

Farther over rode three more horsemen, advancing slowly in the same general direction. He wondered if they belonged to the main party, were simply an offshoot following a wider course, or if they were separate—an entirely different group. He wondered, too, as to their identities; would it be George Cole and a posse already on his trail? It was likely. Stella could have freed herself by now, reached the lawman and voiced

her accusations. Thanks to her, Cole was on the move. Cole—
and maybe the Vengadors.

Bitterness surged up in him, and a quiet anger. The hell
with them. He had the jump on them, whoever they were.
And he'd hold his lead. He could afford an hour or so to find
food to fill his belly, and then he'd move on.

The gray-green valley below simmered in the heat. A mile
ahead crows were wheeling about, and beyond them he saw
the low, squat outlines of a small house. It stood in a
clearing a short distance from the river. A strip of assorted
colors indicating a housewife's washing hung across one end
of the yard. A homesteader, well isolated; hopefully he had
heard nothing of matters in Sacramento Springs.

He rode off the bush-studded mesa at the next erosion, and
dropped into the valley floor. It was cooler; the broad-spread-
ing cottonwoods created oases of shade, and the wild grass
underfoot absorbed some of the wilting heat.

On level ground he looked again to the north. He could see
neither group of riders now. The intervening hills and ridges
blocked them from view.

He wound through the trees; black sage surrounded him,
and scraggy primrose bushes bright with red, yellow, and
faded pink flowers. Drawing closer to the clearing he heard
children's shrill voices. He slowed from habit, allowing time
for the homesteader to become aware of his presence as he
neared the sagging house.

As he passed the children, three boys and two small girls
with their curling hair in white rag pigtails, he winked. They
fell silent, returning his glance with blank stares.

A pen containing a goat and a dozen chickens ran the
breadth of the makeshift structure. Two dogs lying near the
open doorway roused themselves, disturbing a cloud of flies
that began to churn about and finally ran through the doorway into the dark interior of the building.

With the dogs observing him warily, Shay drew to a halt
before the opening. A woman appeared; pools of sweat lay
thick on her ebony cheeks. She greeted him with the same
wooden expression displayed by her offspring.

Jim touched the brim of his hat. "Morning. Your husband
home?"

The woman turned away. Moments later the huge figure of

a man, who had plainly been aroused from a midday nap, blocked the entrance. An ancient double-barreled shotgun hung in the crook of his arm.

"Yes, sir?" he said in the servile, suspicious tone bred by generations of slavery in the Deep South.

"On my way to the border," Jim said. "Run out of grub. Was wondering if I might get a little from you. I'm able to pay."

The big Negro hesitated. After a moment he placed the shotgun against the wall inside the doorway. Unsmiling, he said, "Ain't got much to offer, mister. Reckon you're welcome, such as it is. Step down, and I'll get Addy to stir up a bite."

Jim sighed gently. He swung off the black and settled stiffly on his feet. Involuntarily he glanced toward the north, then grinned wryly. Hell, he could spare an hour.

11

"Name's Saul . . . Saul Crook," the homesteader said, hesitating to extend his hand.

Shay thrust forth his. "Glad to know you. I'm——" He paused for a second. "I'm Rogers. Jim Rogers." He grinned, oddly embarrassed by the lie.

Saul's huge fingers closed about Shay's. "Sure pleased to know you, Mr. Rogers——"

"Jim."

"Yes, sir, Mr. Jim. Step inside out of the sun. Mighty hot for a man to be traveling. Wife'll whup up some vittles right away."

The heat inside the low-roofed structure was only a little less intense than outside; a fire blazed in a small cast-iron cookstove that stood in one corner. The house had two rooms; one for sleeping; the other, a combination kitchen, dining, and living room. The furniture was made from odds and ends of lumber, crates, and packing boxes. Everything was clean.

Crook pointed to a chair, cowhide stretched over a wooden framework, as his wife watched from the entry to the bedroom.

"This here's Mr. Rogers, Addy. He's needing something to eat. Told him you'd whup up a bite."

The woman moved slowly toward the stove. "Got nothing 'cepting hoecakes."

"They're powerful good," Saul said quickly. "She makes them with eggs and goat milk."

60

"Be fine," Jim assured him, settling into the chair. "Don't need to go to much trouble. Appreciate it if you'll make a few extra cakes for me to take along," he added.

"Ain't got nothing for your horse," Saul said.

"He'll do fine," Jim answered. "Expect I ought to give him a little water, though."

"You stay right there, Mr. Rogers. The boy can do it."

Saul stepped to the doorway and called instructions to the eldest of his children. Clearly pleased to have a visitor, he came back into the room. "Boy'll take care of your horse, Mr. Rogers. You riding far?"

Jim thought for a moment. "Guess you can say I'm just drifting," he said. He pointed to the shotgun. "Trouble?"

Saul Crook's face lengthened. "A smidgen. Once in a while somebody comes along that don't like us nigras living here. Reckon it could be worse."

Addy turned her head, gave her husband a hard, hopeless glance, then resumed mixing the batter.

"Addy ain't so pleasured with it, but I keep telling her we're doing better'n most folks like us. We got our own land and this here house. And things ain't like they was before the war. We didn't have nothing then. Just pure nothing. My children ain't never going to know what it was like before the war."

Addy spoke then for the second time since Jim had ridden up. "Your children ain't going to have nothing—that's what they ain't," she said flatly. "We're living out here like the wild things."

"But it's our life we're living, I keep telling you that. We ain't doing for nobody but ourselves. And what we do is our own."

Addy sighed loudly. At length she handed Shay a tin plate with four hoecakes on it. They were excellent. The homesteader, hunched against the wall, watched, his broad teeth showing behind his lips as he awaited Jim's verdict.

"Best I ever ate," Shay said, smiling, and Crook relaxed.

"You homestead this place?" Jim asked.

"Yes, sir," Saul replied. "Got us a whole hundred and sixty acres. Man I knowed in the war helped me get it."

"You ain't doing much with it," Addy said pointedly.

"Doing the best I can. But they's things I don't know about —things I got to be learning."

"What are you raising?" Shay asked. His eyes strayed to Addy who was placing four more cakes on the glowing stove.

"Got a corn patch. And they's turnips and peppers growing good. Couldn't have no luck with 'taters. Then we got chickens and the goat."

"A hundred and sixty acres of ground, and you're using maybe one acre," Addy said, not raising her head. "Pure, shameful waste, all that ground and doing nothing but sprouting weeds."

"Takes time. . . ."

"More'n we got. Time you get around to doing something, we'll be too old to do nothing. Children's going to have nothing. Plain nothing."

"They got a place to live and grow up. That's more'n lotsa folk's children's got."

"More to living than growing up. . . ."

"Maybe, but growing up on your own land without somebody always hollering at you—do this, and do that—is mighty good. You know I'm telling you for true, Addy."

She brushed at her brow with a forearm. "I know it," she said, her tone relenting. "Only seems we're getting nowhere. Seems we ought to have more. Owning ourselves is fine, but there ought to be more to it."

Saul stirred angrily. "You're still harping about us living with Mr. Barndollar—that's what you're doing. You're still flopping that around in your head."

"I sure am. And I ain't quitting. Would be real fine for us and the children."

Crook rose impatiently. He wheeled to Jim. "Maybe you can tell us what we ought to do, Mr. Rogers. Maybe you can tell us what's right and what ain't. Man who helped me get this here homestead was by to see us. Got hisself a ranch way off in the hills. . . . Lives all alone. Made me a offer to come live there. I'd be doing chores and working the farm, sort of helping like. Addy would do the cooking and housekeeping—"

"And the children wouldn't be growing up like the wild things," Addy broke in. "We'd be having us plenty to eat, a dry place to sleep . . . and there'd be money for spending. . . ."

"Five dollars a month," Saul said scornfully. "I can make that much on a few bushels of corn——"

"If you've got a few bushels."

Saul extended his hands, palms upward, to Shay. "What you figure I ought to do, Mr. Rogers? Stay here or go to Mr. Barndollar's place?"

Jim got to his feet and sauntered to the doorway. Nothing could be seen beyond the rim of close-standing hills except the layers of heat pressing firmly upon the land. He faced Saul.

"Advantages to both sides," he said. "You've got a fine place here. . . . In time it could be made to pay. But it will be all your worry and responsibility—and it'll take plenty of hard work."

"Ain't ascared of that. Used to it."

"Expect you are, but it takes planning and such. On the other hand, you'd have an easy time of it working for this friend of yours. You'd have security, and I expect that's worth a good deal—especially to a woman with children to bring up."

"Only thing, wouldn't be us living our lives. We'd be living and working for somebody else."

"That's true—and it's a choice you'll have to make. We're all faced with a decision like that now and then, and there's no good rule to go by. Important thing is once you've made the choice, live with it. Don't ever regret it. Keep remembering you did what you figured was the right thing, no matter how it turns out."

Saul wagged his head dolefully. "Sure seems a man has to learn a lot, just about living."

Shay clucked sympathetically. The hour was about up, and it was time he moved on.

"How long have you folks been around here?"

Saul, again leaning against the wall, and staring moodily at his broad, powerful hands, lifted his head. " 'Most four years. Maybe the place don't look it, but I done all I could to fix it up."

"When you start with nothing, it takes a long time," Jim said. "You acquainted with the Slaussons?"

"Slaussons?" the homesteader repeated. "Reckon not. Don't know many folks. They close by?"

"Probably twenty miles or so on down the valley."

"Sure don't recollect ever seeing them."

"How about an old man with a yellow beard? Drives a team of mules. Don't know his name."

Saul's dark face brightened. "You meaning Mr. Barndollar?"

Jim Shay drew to sudden attention. "I don't know his name . . . only what he looks like."

Sure does sound like Mr. Barndollar. He's the friend I was telling you about. . . . Helped me get this here place."

Shay's nerves tightened. "When did you last see him?"

"Two, maybe three days ago," Saul replied, looking at Addy. "Was the day he come offering me that job. Had been down Las Cruces way, he said."

His voice strained, Jim said. "Where does Barndollar live?"

"East of here," Saul said. "Over in what they calls the Loco Hills country."

12

Evidently Barndollar did his trading in Las Cruces, a settlement farther south; that would accóunt for no one in Sacramento Springs being acquainted with him.

"You going to see Mr. Barndollar?" Saul asked.

Shay nodded. "Be moving out right away."

The homesteader frowned, rose to his feet. "Powerful hot out there."

"Know that. But it can't be helped. Important that I overtake this Barndollar soon as I can."

He was at the widest part of the Jornada. There were shorter, less wicked routes across its burning breadth lying to the north and to the south, but he could not afford the time required to double back or to continue on down the valley.

"I'll need extra water. Think you can rustle me up another canteen of some kind? Bottle will do."

Saul began to dig about in a box that stood in the corner. "Was a molasses jug somewheres. . . ."

"Anything will do," Shay said, and stepped out into the withering sunshine. He crossed to the black, grazing lazily in the shade. Leading him to the wooden tub at the pump he allowed him to drink again.

Saul emerged from the house with the molasses jug and a sack of hoecakes. "Man sure oughtn't to be traveling out there this time of day, Mr. Rogers," he said doubtfully. "Ain't nobody goes across, less'n it's dark."

Jim squinted at the sun. "Few hours won't hurt me. Be night by the time I reach the worst part."

Saul wagged his head. "You sure want to see Mr. Barndollar mighty bad."

Shay nodded. Addy came into the yard. Turning to Saul, Jim handed two dollars to the homesteader.

"Obliged to you for everything."

Saul looked at the coins. His thick lips broke into a wide, toothy smile, and then immediately he sobered.

"No, sir, Mr. Rogers. I can't be taking no money for hospitality. It ain't right."

"Keep it," Jim said, swinging onto the saddle. "Been worth plenty to me . . . the meal and the talk both." He shifted his glance to Addy. "You're a fine cook. Hope things work out for you."

She nodded gravely, and nudged Saul. "You going to have him tell Mr. Barndollar something?"

Crook shuffled uneasily. "Well, I just ain't sure yet," he mumbled. Raising his eyes to Shay, he added, "You tell him I'm thinking on it, if'n you don't mind."

"I'll tell him," Jim said. "But maybe you can tell him yourself. Things go right, we'll be back through here in a couple of days."

Saul grinned happily; Addy's frown deepened. Shay swung the gelding around. He winked at the stair-step row of children, touched the brim of his hat to the homesteader and his wife, and was off. At the end of the cleared hard-pack, he threw a last glance to the north, saw no boil of dust anywhere against the molten sky, and began to ride in earnest.

He struck a direct course for the river; the blazing sun flayed his back and shoulders with merciless intensity. He could expect this for several hours.

At the Rio Grande, he dipped down off the bank into the siltladen water. The gelding plodded slowly through it.

"Make the most of it," Shay murmured absently, looking ahead to the parched portion of the riverbed that rose above the normal channel. "You won't be walking through water again for a spell."

The black reached the far bank, climbed up, and moved on. There were times of the year when the Rio flowed rich and full across this section, too, and could be a half-mile-wide

sheet of roily, swirling water. Such periods, however, were of
brief duration. Ordinarily the river here was as he saw it
now, a narrow, shallow, sluggish strip.

Gaining the alkali-streaked east bank proper, Jim urged
the gelding onto the belt-high shoulder. He left the willows
and salt cedars behind, and broke out onto dry, sandy ground.
He was in unfamiliar country here; he had ridden through
only once or twice before. But an eastward course would take
him to the edge of the Jornada, and from there he could
establish exact bearings.

One thing he did know. Sixty miles of desolation lay between the river and the Oscura Mountains, the first break in
that blistered world of the Jornada, and the Oscuras offered
little other than a change from the deadly monotony of the
cruel desert to lifting hills. They were known to be dry most
of the time. But Jim had his canteen and the gallon jug
Saul Crook had provided. And Barndollar would be carrying
a supply of water. He could refill his containers when he
caught up with the rancher.

The last of the gray-green saltbush and stunted junipers
fell away, and the broad, gleaming desert stretched before
him. The sun was a stabbing flame at his back again.

The Loco Hills country, where Barndollar was said to live,
lay due east, well beyond the dim bluish haze of the Capitan
Mountains. To Shay's left rose the Oscuras, with Oscura Peak
at the northernmost point, Burro Peak about midway, and the
highest of the three, Salinas, at the southern end. On past
Salinas stretched the San Andres Range. He must be careful not to veer toward them.

Barndollar would have taken the lower trail across the
Jornada. It converged with the northern route near the
base of the Oscuras, and together they wound on between
Burro and Salinas peaks, to continue through the rugged
canyon country of Black Mountain and eventually break
out onto the plains far to the east.

Shay stood now in the mouth of the V formed by the
converging trails, with the full width of the Jornada before
him. He thought little of the fact that he was about to dare
this murderous land at its worst; he concentrated only on
his plan to keep a middle course, with Burro Peak always
on his left, Salinas to his right, the Oscuras to the north,

and the San Andres Range to the south. This should bring him out on the heels of Barndollar's mules.

He sheltered his eyes to look back once more, trying to locate dust. He could see nothing in the white-hot haze. Then he touched the gelding with his heels. The big horse moved out slowly across the loose, hot sand.

Within the hour the sun had sucked Jim dry. He began to lean forward on the saddle, head down, while the burning rays lanced deep into his body, sapping him of strength, almost of consciousness. A wind was rising slowly, moving in from the south, from across a hundred miles of torrid, glinting sand; it stirred the countless creosote bushes, worried the chollas and half-buried mesquites, but brought no relief.

As the hours passed it grew steadily in force. Dust began to drift, to spin crazily in tight, choking funnels, disturbing the sullen layers of heat. Shay dug about in his saddlebags, and found an old undershirt. He wrapped it about his face, covering his nose and mouth and leaving only his red-rimmed eyes visible. The cloth almost suffocated him, but it did keep the fine, irritating dust particles from his throat.

The gelding plodded on stolidly. The wind graduated to a gale. The dust disappeared, spinning away to higher levels of wind currents, and in its place came gusts of sand, sharp and cutting. And still the relentless, merciless sun broiled his back and shoulders.

Sundown came finally, but there was no surcease of heat, only a slow fading of the searing fire in his shoulders, neck, and back. He twisted about on the saddle and stared bleakly at the western horizon, a long, narrow band of red-gold and purest yellow seen through a brown haze. He grinned through the grit in his teeth, a gaunt-faced, hollow-eyed wolf of a man. "I've made it this far . . . I'll go the rest of the way!" he shouted at the vanished sun.

But now there was more wind.

It had increased as the day died. Suddenly it was a furious, blasting scourge, heavy with knife-edged sand, burning with heat stored by the land during the long, sun-charged hours. The black began to show fear. Jim tried to veer north, put a stinging whiplash to his black's rump. He fought to keep the horse in line, pulling him back, cursing him wildly for his stubbornness, cursing himself for having no spurs. He dared not close his smarting eyes, give them rest and perhaps sleep; the instant he relaxed his steady pressure on the gelding's reins, the horse would swing off course and drift with the wind. And that would be fatal.

"Blow! Goddamit—blow!" Shay yelled suddenly in a fit of frenzied exasperation.

He continued to swear, to curse the night, the never-ending heat, the wild gusts, the limitless miles that still lay ahead—anything he could think of to keep his thoughts channeled to the task that was before him. Occasionally he would allow the gelding to wheel about and rest, with the frightful wind at his hindquarters. Regularly he would peer ahead through half-closed eyes to assure himself of his position.

With the coming of night and the storm of dust and sand, the two peaks were obscured, and at times he could not locate them. But always he could make out the shadowy bulk of the Oscuras and keep them properly placed until the towering Salinas or the somewhat lower Burro Peak emerged through the gloom.

The wind redoubled, and it became a struggle even to keep the gelding moving, to hold himself in the saddle. He rode folded forward, right hand keeping the black's head pointed for the peaks, left clamped tight to the horn. The undershirt was still about his face, knotted tight to prevent its being carried away, and his hat was pulled so low on his head that his temples throbbed. Except for the times when he checked his course, he kept his eyes closed. The insides of the lids felt like raw meat.

At midnight the wind slackened, mercifully dwindling to a stiff blow. A short time later Jim reached a low bluff. Earlier it would have been a godsend, now it was merely a convenient break. He rode in behind it and dismounted. Salinas Peak still rose to his right, Burro to the left. He shrugged, wondering vaguely how he had managed to stay on course during that hell of shifting sand.

He was stiff and cramped from the rigid position he had maintained for so long. It felt good to stand, to stamp his feet, although weariness made it an effort. He unwound the dirty undershirt from his head, shook it out thoroughly and stuffed it into a pocket. He was thirsty, and he helped himself

to a long swallow from the molasses jug. The canteen was
almost empty.

The black whickered anxiously. Shay took out the old undershirt again, soaked it heavily, and squeezed it dry into the
gelding's mouth. He repeated the process twice, and then
used the damp cloth to clean the horse's eyes, nostrils, and
lips.

After a half hour of rest Jim moved on. The desert was
calm now, glowing with an eerie, cold beauty in the silver
light of the stars and a high-riding moon. But it was an
empty world, devoid of all life except the stark cactus growths,
the starved, scorched saltbushes and leafless snakeweed. And
where before there had been searing, breathless heat, there
were now the beginnings of a subtle, biting chill.

Jim Shay drew on his brush jacket. He was about midway
to Black Mountain, he guessed. Somewhere beyond it he
should catch sight of Barndollar. If not, he would simply
have to keep on and trail him the entire distance to the Loco
Hills.

The chill deepened as he rode on. At times he would
dismount and walk ahead of the gelding to keep his blood
circulating. Anger would surge through him and he would
curse furiously, blasting a country that baked a man crisp in
the day, turned him to ice at night.

In darkness he reached the junction of the trails and
pressed on across the broad swale that lay between the two
peaks. Both he and the black moved from sheer reflex now;
the point of total exhaustion was not far off.

Later, at the edge of a vast, ragged black malpais bed, Shay
waited for sunrise. When it came, a bursting fan of orange
and salmon fingers, he resumed the journey. Within an hour,
on the crest of a steep rise, he stopped once more. The long
slopes of Black Mountain lay dead ahead.

Twisting about, he looked to his back trail. He grinned,
cracking his crusted, dry lips. The Jornada was behind him.

13

After a short rest, he rode on toward the mountain. A cold, flowing spring lay at the foot of the pine-studded slopes—or should, but knowing the land and its whimsies, he had learned never to take such things for granted. The growth in the hollow appeared a healthy green, however, and, his hopes rising, he urged the worn black on.

They climbed the gradual grade. Abruptly the gelding caught the smell of water, and his head came up. His pace changed to a shambling trot. Once on the level where the spring could be seen bursting from beneath a rocky shelf, the horse broke into a lope, and a short time later they halted at the spongy edge of the pool. Shay dropped from the saddle as the black lowered his head and began to suck in drafts of the cold water.

Lying on his belly, Jim plunged his head below the surface of the quiet pool, reveling in the cool freshness. Then he took one of Addy Crook's hoecakes from the sack, and ate his breakfast. The gelding, his thirst satisfied, stood nearby cropping at the short, sweet grass that grew abundantly around the spring.

Shay spent the better part of an hour sprawled full-length on the soft earth; then he began to stroll about. He was stiff from the long, tense night, and the muscles of his back and legs still ached. Exercise should relieve the pain —but the nagging need to keep moving never left him.

He climbed a short distance up the slope and out onto a

rocky brow that overlooked the flat below. To the west the Jornada stretched on beyond the foothills. Already it was a shimmering, glistening heat band. Even at this early hour, the temperature near its center would be soaring to withering heights.

Although he expected to see no riders, Jim looked for dust rolls. The trail between the peaks was empty, and what he could see of the two trails beyond, one angling southward, the other north, revealed no travelers.

George Cole and his posse, if that was who the riders had been, were likely still searching the valley along the Rio Grande for him. He wondered if the old lawman, learning from Saul Crook of his visit and subsequent trip onto the Jornada, would follow. Jim decided Cole was the sort of man who would.

Back at the pond, he examined the soft ooze thoughtfully. Barndollar should have paused there to rest and water his mules. Finding prints might give him an idea of how far ahead the rancher would be.

At the south end of the pool, in the deep mud, he discovered deer tracks, the small, cloven hoof marks pressed deep and sharply defined. Not far from those were the neat spherical patterns of a cougar's tracks—two solitary prints, as though the big cat had approached the waterhole, seen something of interest or danger, and retreated.

On the opposite bank he found the narrow, clean-cut indentations of an iron-tired wagon wheel. Shay squatted, touched the edges of the slices and found them firm. Barndollar—if it had been Barndollar—had been there the previous day. Likely he had spent the afternoon at the spring recuperating, and then moved on after darkness fell.

Shay continued to prowl. He came to a cluster of prints where the team had been picketed. The droppings and the small size of the tracks confirmed his belief that mules had been there. The droppings would be at least fifteen hours old, he judged.

Then as he turned away he caught sight of more hoofprints—a great many more. Fifteen or twenty horses, he guessed. The riders had swung in from the opposite slope, paused just outside the hollow where the spring flowed.

Why had they not come in for water?

Alarm began to stir within Jim Shay. He went to his knees to examine the tracks, not so definite and clear-cut here on firmer soil as were those in the soft mud. Some of the horses had not been shod; others had. It could mean only one thing—Apaches.

He came upright in a quick lurch, hurriedly glancing along the encircling slopes. He saw only the gradually heating rocks, the stalwart pines marching rigidly down the mountainsides, the tough scrub cedars and twisted junipers crouched low where they clung to the mountain. A solitary eagle circled high above the canyons. Jim stood for a long moment watching the graceful soaring of the winged king, while the remarks made by Rue Gilman and George Cole about the Indians came back to his mind.

There was ground for fear. The Federal Government's Indian colonization scheme had failed. Colonel Kit Carson's labors to subdue and round up the fierce, warlike Mescalero Apaches and quarrelsome Navajos and place them in the Bosque Redondo had been in vain. In only a few years the Apaches had fled the reservation, unable to get along with either themselves, the Navajos, or the whites.

They had split into numerous small tribes, taken refuge in the rugged mountains, and defied all efforts to dislodge them. With that the Washington authorities had thrown up their hands in despair. They had sent the Navajos back to their ancestral hunting grounds west of the Rio Grande and hoped that the Mescaleros would behave.

They had been disappointed. The Apaches, never ones to pursue a sedentary existence, scornful of the agricultural life, which they considered degrading and an insult to their history as a proud, warring people, fell swiftly into the old pattern. They became ruthless marauders, hunting the wild country, striking hard at isolated ranchers and out-of-the-way homesteaders. Solitary travelers and small parties en route to distant settlements became their favorite prey.

The army, stripped to a minimum after the close of the War between the States, and concentrated in three or four specific areas in the territory, was finding itself almost helpless in a fight against ghostly, half-naked warriors who were here one day, at some removed point the next.

Barndollar would be a succulent prize indeed, Jim Shay

thought, as worry grew within him. The Apaches would find everything to their liking: an old man, alone, in a wagon loaded with supplies, pulled by their choicest meat—mules.

Shay whirled. He located the tracks of the wagon again, and followed them to where they swung onto the road. A dozen yards later the Apaches had moved in behind; the hoofprints of their ponies could be seen stamped atop the narrow ribbons left in the dust by the wheels.

Jim hurried to the gelding. Mounting, he lashed the big horse into a lope up the trail. He was a good many hours behind Barndollar and the Indians; he prayed he could catch up before the bloodthirsty renegades could harm the old rancher.

Around noon, in a shaded dell just off trail, he paused to breathe the gelding and eat another hoecake. It had been a gradual climb all the way from the spring, and he had pushed the gelding hard. A horse with less bottom could never have stood the punishment, but the black was a powerful brute, needing only brief periods of rest in which to regain his strength.

Anxiety robbed Shay of his hunger, and after a few minutes he tossed the remainder of the cake to a half a dozen chattering camp robbers who had come in close to investigate. Mounting up, he pushed on.

Near three o'clock, with the gelding plastered with sweat and caked with dust, with his own body bathed in salty moisture, he saw tendrils of black smoke rising from a canyon a mile off trail.

He thundered down the grade at the gelding's best, swung off when he reached the level, and cut across open country, heading for the telltale columns. Fear obsessed him now; he wasted no more time in speculation, or in searching for Barndollar's wagon tracks. The rancher would be an irresistible magnet to the roving warriors, and Jim Shay knew that he was drawing to the end of his search for the old man.

The canyon was farther off the road than it had appeared. He was in a land of deep ravines, gashed by lateral washes. The slopes were steep and rock-covered. Brush clawed at the gelding's legs, tore at Shay's clothing. Twice they almost fell on the uneven ground, but Shay raced on, ignoring the black's labored breathing, and forcing him to continue.

He had heard no gunshots; from that he took some hope. Rifle reports carried for long distances in the hills, and as he had heard none since he had reached Black Mountain, he felt there was a possibility that Barndollar was yet alive. The Apaches could be interesting themselves only in his cargo and his sleek, fat mules.

Or he could already be dead.

Jim Shay hammered grimly at the black's ribs with his heels, driving him on toward the edge of the canyon, now only a hundred yards away. The smoke strings had thinned, indicating that whatever had been set afire had about burned itself down. That, too, was ominous.

Just short of the rim Shay pulled to a halt. Anchoring the heaving black to a clump of prickly gooseberry, he bellied his way to the edge. He looked down into the narrow gorge— and recoiled.

"The goddam bloody bastards!" he groaned, a wave of sickness sweeping through him.

Barndollar lay spread-eagled on the sand of a small clearing. Dark patches all over his body marked the presence of numerous knife thrusts. The wounds had been made just deep enough to cause free bleeding, prolonging the pleasure of the torture. But the rancher was dead now. He lay on his back, yellow beard outthrust, sightless eyes staring into the burning sky.

There were sixteen Apaches. All were dark, fierce-looking braves dressed in breechcloths or ragged white drawers. Some wore shirts, others bared their gleaming copper torsos to the sun; all had the traditional band of cloth about their heads to hold their coarse black hair in place. . . . And each carried a rifle, many the latest repeating model.

They had unloaded the wagon, then burned it. The boxes of supplies had been dumped onto the ground, the contents ransacked. What was unwanted had been tossed into the flames. Both mules had been slaughtered. Chunks of the bloody meat were being passed out to each brave.

An argument broke out between two men over some item taken from Barndollar's body. The distance was too great for Jim to determine what it might be, but the bickering rose quickly to a feverish heat. Finally, a squat, graying warrior astride a fine-looking sorrel shouted something. Both men turned away, sullen and angry. The smaller of the pair suddenly drew his knife and lunged toward Barndollar's lifeless body. With two slashes he ripped open the rancher's belly.

A great laugh went up as Jim Shay lay back, his skin crawling. Helpless, he lay there, beating his fist against the solid earth. *Damn the bloodthirsty bastards! Damn them all to hell! Why couldn't he have got there sooner? Where the hell was the stinking army? Why weren't they on the job?* Seething, he looked over the rim again. The Apaches were moving off.

He watched them thread their way single file up a narrow trail on the far side of the canyon and disappear one by one into the pines and spruces. When the last one had gone, and there was nothing in the gorge but death, he got up and made his way back to the gelding.

An odd thought passed through his mind: Saul Crook could stop fretting now. He no longer had to make a choice.

And Jim Shay's only hope—the one man who could prove him innocent of the Slausson murders—was gone.

14

He mounted the gelding again and picked his way along the rim of the canyon until he found a wash down which he could gain the floor. The black liked neither the look nor the smell of things, and Shay halted a dozen yards away. Leaving the horse securely tied, he crossed to where Barndollar's body lay. Death had indeed been a merciful deliverance for the rancher.

He hunted up a short length of wood, part of the charred wagon bed, and scooped out a shallow grave. Salvaging a bit of burned blanket he brushed away the gathering flies, and wrapped the man as best he could. He dragged him into the hollow and piled a high mound of earth and stones over him, hoping it would be sufficient to keep the animals away. Then he took the length of board he had used as a shovel and, with his knife and a bit of charcoal, fashioned a grave marker.

He mounted the gelding in glum silence and headed back for the road. There was nothing to do but return to the valley and to dig up some other means of proving his innocence. The Slausson farm . . . that would be the logical place to start. Rue Gilman had not bothered to look for evidence, for signs of someone else that Sunday when he had ridden onto the scene. He had simply assumed the worst insofar as Jim was concerned, arrested him promptly for the crime, and taken him on to Sacramento Springs.

No one would be at the farm, he was certain. It had come out at the trial that Slausson's relatives all lived in the East, that his wife had a brother but his whereabouts were unknown.

It meant crossing the Jornada again. Jim accepted that fact stolidly. Maybe it wouldn't be so bad this time. It might not be so hot, possibly the damn wind wouldn't whip up and blow as though the gates of hell had just swung open. But he knew this to be wishful thinking.

He would be getting a late start, he realized, as the gelding labored over the slopes. That would be of some help; the sun would be down. He would not be entirely across by dawn, and the heat would catch him long before he reached the Rio Grande—but that was preferable to staring into the sun hour after hour.

He could save a little time by angling off to the south side of Black Mountain, thus taking a shortcut to the intersection with the southern road. It eventually crossed the river somewhere near Slausson's. The trail skirted the northern tip of the San Andres, and they would serve as his landmark.

He filled his canteen and the jug at the spring, and ate the last of the hoecakes. Fresh meat would be welcome—a rabbit or one of the squirrels he had seen scampering about in the pines, but he would be a fool to use his gun on one. When there were Apaches on the loose, a man did nothing to draw their attention.

At dark he moved out. He had benefited little from the short rest. The continuing pressure and strain, the long hours in the saddle with no satisfactory sleep, the scant food, were wearing him down. He could have delayed his journey for a night, possibly even for the entire length of the following day. But the ominous knowledge that Apaches lurked in the area ruled that out.

Now, as the black wound his way down the long slope, Jim's muscles went slack. His shoulders drooped as his head sank lower onto his chest. He couldn't remember when he had last enjoyed a full meal or a night's sleep in a bed.

The recrossing of the Jornada was no better and no worse than before. He reached the Rio Grande late in the morning, feverish from the searing heat, a worn, sweat-soaked ghost of a man just able mechanically to sit upright on a staggering horse. His face had assumed a lean, wolfish look. His eyes were swelled shut, his lips twin lines of dust-filled cracks. He was covered by a fine gray powder that clung to his brows, his hair and beard, and imparted a hoary aspect to all of him.

The exhausted gelding halted of his own accord in the muddy water and immediately lowered his head. Shay, roused from his stupor by the cessation of motion, looked about, dazed. The water glinted dully before him. A croaking sound escaped his throat. He started to dismount, but his legs were cramped and he had no control over them. He fell full-length into the silty current.

He lay there, soaking, recovering slowly while the gelding took his fill. After a time Shay dragged himself to his feet and clambered onto the bank, rivulets pouring from his clothing. He sank into the coolness of the willows and bunch grass, and lay back. He was vaguely conscious of the black moving by him and beginning to graze.

Shay slept for an hour. Waking, he sat up and gazed about in thick, stupid wonder. After a few moments he cupped a hand over his still smarting eyes and looked out onto the sweltering breast of the Jornada. The brilliant glare dazzled him, and he closed his lids to shut it out as pain jabbed through his head. He had crossed that blistering hell once more.

He had no idea of his position. If the black had stayed true on course he should be somewhere near the Slausson farm, but from the bed of the river he could determine nothing. His range of vision was hampered by the dense brush, the salt cedars and cottonwoods. He would have to find higher ground.

He rested in the shade for another hour, and then, reluctantly, led the gelding away from the river. Once again his appetite was clamoring for attention.

He trailed the gelding behind him through the dense brush until they reached a thinning in the rank growth, and there he swung to the saddle. From where he now sat he could see hills farther west—and beyond them a line of rose-colored buttes. They appeared familiar, but they gave him no definite clue as to where he might be; he still needed an overall look at the valley. Veering the black left, he headed for the tallest of the near hills.

He realized that a full-fledged man hunt must be underway by now, and Cole would be getting plenty of help, wanted or not, from the Vengadors. The thought of moving on to the Mexican border seemed more and more logical. If he stayed, and tried to fight it out, his chances of winning would be almost too slim to calculate. But as before, when the thought of running passed through his mind, he brushed it aside. Somewhere—somehow—he would find the proof he must have. . . . And then he would be free.

The black reached the hill and made his way to the crest. Squinting into the brilliance, Shay scanned the long rectangle of green below. Thankfulness surged through him. The Slausson place was less than a mile distant. The gelding had veered during the wild, tempestuous hours of the night— fortunately in the right direction.

Twenty miles to the south three riders, a woman and two men, drew to a halt on another hilltop and studied the long-reaching, gully-scarred flats far below. From their position they could see for miles across an expanse marked only by clumps of creosote bush, seared, stark cholla, and sand-whipped mesquite. Nothing moved on that desolate plain baking in the fiery sun.

"He ain't down there," Dave Lund said. His voice dragged, and he was sweat-stained, dusty, and hollow-eyed; he showed the marks of continual hours in the saddle.

Sanford was no better off. A tougher man, he reflected the strain less, but appeared to be at the ragged end of his temper. "The son of a bitch had to go somewhere," he said, turning to the girl. "What do you think, Stell?"

She did not take her gaze from the flat. "I think," she said slowly, "we've overrun him. He's still behind us."

She was dressed in a coarse shirt, open down the front in the interest of coolness rather than sex, a pair of faded Levi's, and knee-high, flat-heeled boots. Under the brim of a stained, low-crowned hat her features were harsh, and streaked with dust and sweat.

"He headed south," Sanford said stubbornly. "Tracks showed that. How the hell could we have overrode him?"

"How the hell couldn't we?" she echoed angrily, waving

a hand at the brush-crowded valley behind them. "You could lose a wagon train in there."

"I'm betting he went east," Lund said, reaching for his canteen. "I'm betting that rider we seen night before last heading out across the Jornada was him." He tipped the canteen vertically and drained it. "Had a hunch all the time it was him."

Sanford flung a glance of disgust at Lund. "If you was so goddamed sure, why didn't you say so then?"

"Didn't say I was sure," Lund replied, his own tone sharpening. "Said I had a hunch. Come on, let's get out of this sun."

Stella did not stir. Still staring out onto the flat, she said, "Doesn't make sense. Why would he cross the Jornada? Lot easier to run for Mexico. And safer."

"Who knows what that bird's thinking?" Lund said. "But I'll bet my share of the thirty thousand he's the one we seen."

Sanford spat. "So what're we doing? Roast here on our butts while he gets further away?"

"We go over him—now," Stella said quietly.

Dave Lund's head came up. "Cross the Jornada in the day?" he said incredulously. "That's crazy, Stell!"

"You want your part of the gold, don't you? Only way you'll get it is go after it—and keep after it until we run him down. If Shay rode east, we've got to do the same."

"But the Jornada! Can't we wait till dark? And we're out of water. And we ain't got no grub."

"Eight, nine hours until dark. He can cover a lot of ground in that much time."

Aaron Sanford, hunched forward on his saddle, his hands resting on the horn, studied the smoky San Andres peaks far to the east. "Be one hell of a ride across there, but I reckon it's got to be done. Only thing bothering me is that maybe it wasn't him. . . . Could've been some stinking pilgrim. . . ."

"Not likely," Stella replied. "Have to be somebody that was in a hurry—somebody anxious to get out of the valley. . . ."

It does sound like him," Lund said, nodding. He mopped sweat from his eyes. "If I had the law, a lynching party, and three mighty unfriendly people riding my tail, I'd take out, too."

Sanford grunted, and heaved upright. "All right, I'm

game. But we'll need grub. And water. Nothing much east of here for a hundred miles. Where'll we stock up?"

Stella pulled her horse about. "The Slausson place. They've got a well, and there ought to be some food laying around we can use."

15

Jim Shay approached the Slausson place from the north. He halted in the dense, bordering windbreak of Osage orange and tamarisk that pocketed the graying, weathered structures, and studied the main house carefully. He remained for several minutes in silent contemplation, certain the property was deserted, but cautious nevertheless.

Finally convinced that there was no one about, he walked the tired black to the barn, which stood a good fifty yards to the rear. Slausson's stock had evidently been stolen or taken over by neighbors, as no cows or horses were in evidence and the gate to the chicken yard stood open.

Ground reining the gelding, Jim entered the cool, shadowy depths of the barn, strangely silent, and gained the first stall. There was grain in the manger, and water. He led the black into the windbreak, tied him securely, and set a bucket before him.

He followed the windbreak along its northern edge until he was abreast of the house, and then quickly crossed the open yard to the rear door. The panel was hooked from the inside. He drew his knife and flipped the catch aside. Stepping inside quickly, he closed the panel and replaced the hook.

He stood in the center of the kitchen and listened. The place lay dead in stuffy silence, its trapped air hot. Shay put down the urge to rummage through the shelves for food. First he must have a thorough look at the house.

He moved quietly into the parlor. This was where he had

found Slausson. The cords used to string him by the thumbs still dangled from the ceiling beams. Standing at the door, he peered through the neatly curtained glass mounted in upper center. The yard beyond lay still and hot in the midday sun.

He passed on into the bedroom with its adjoining storage area, a closet almost as large as the room itself. Everything was as he had last seen it. Only the Slaussons' bodies had been removed.

Satisfied, he returned to the kitchen. In the oven of the square, nickel-trimmed Old Homestead cookstove he found a pan of stale biscuits, prepared that Sunday morning by Mrs. Slausson. Among the supplies on the shelves he discovered a quart-sized Mason jar of pickled peaches, and another filled with slices of dried beef. He could find no coffee.

He sat down at the table to his meal, wolfing the food hungrily. Then he eased his thirst with a dipper of tepid water from a tin bucket near the door. He must remember to refill his canteen before he rode out, he thought, placing two remaining biscuits in his pockets.

Next he began a minute investigation of the house. He went from room to room. There *had* to be something in the way of a clue.

From time to time he glanced through a window. The two groups of riders he had noted that afternoon when he crossed the Jornada could still be in the area. George Cole would not have given up; as for the second party—if it had been unallied with Cole's group—he was not so sure. Lynch mobs ordinarily cooled off fast when their intended victim proved difficult to catch.

He eventually gave up on the house. At the door he considered going over the yard carefully. He should wait until night when he would not be so noticeable, but sundown was hours away, and he didn't like the idea of spending any more time around here than was absolutely necessary. Too, darkness would hinder the search. He would have to take the risk.

He found the front door unlocked and stepped out onto the small square of warped boards that served as a porch. At that moment he heard the distant click of a horseshoe striking against a stone, and then the dry squeak of leather.

He whirled and leaped back through the doorway, his nerves suddenly taut steel wires.

The riders rode in from the south. He knew them all.

Surprise rocked through him at seeing them together. Then understanding dawned upon him: Stella had the two outlaws working for her. She had hired them to help run him down, still convinced that he had Cal Garrick's mythical gold. They looked as though they had been in the saddle for days—as indeed they must have been if they had started to search for him not long after he had left Stella's house.

They could have been the three riders he had seen on the ridge. If so, then the other group of horsemen had been George Cole and his posse, and there had been no connection.

Shay looked quickly for a safe place to hide. He was trapped in this room with no place to go except out—and that he could not do until he knew what they had in mind. . . .

He watched them dismount, their movements stiff and set. Sanford removed his hat and absently dusted it against his knee. There was a dark bruise on the gunman's face just above the cheekbone—a souvenir of the blow Jim had given him that night in the brush at the foot of the Ladrones.

Dave Lund moved up, limping because of his restricted, painful muscles. He rubbed at his whiskered jaw and yawned.

"Sure could use some shut-eye," he said, slanting a glance at Stella. "Can't see how it'll make a lot of difference if we wait for dark."

"Makes plenty of difference," Stella said in the patient, weary tone of one worn to a frazzle by constant bickering. She stiffened suddenly, came about and faced him. "Dave—you want to give up on Shay? You ready to forget your part of the gold? If so—say it now. Here will be as good a place as any for you to call it quits."

Lund shrugged, cocked his head. "Now, Stell, I only—"

"I mean it!" she said angrily. "All you've done from the start is bitch and bellyache. Makes no difference to me if you want out—both of you. So far you've managed to do nothing but mess things up, anyway. I'd probably be better off if you'd both move on and let me handle this by myself."

Jim had assumed at first that Stella had merely hired the outlaws to aid her in finding him; it sounded now as though there were more to it.

Sanford shifted his weight. "Sure, sure," he drawled. "I got me a picture of you riding out across the Jornada all by your lonesome, chasing after Shay. You ain't that dumb."

Stella brushed at her face impatiently, succeeded only in moving the dust from one spot to another. "Don't think I couldn't do it," she snapped. "You'll never see the day when I can't do anything any man can do!"

"Sure, sure," Sanford said again, soothingly. "Could be she's a better man than either of us, eh, Dave?"

Lund grinned salaciously. "Could be—only, Lord be praised, she's sure built different."

Stella's eyes snapped. "We're losing time. What's it going to be, Dave?"

Lund sobered, and stared at the ground. "Maybe we ought to pull out, Aaron. Maybe we just ought to head south and drop the whole goddam thing in her lap—she's so all-fired smart. I ain't so sure there's gold, anyway."

Stella tugged at the waistband of her Levi's. "Go right ahead, mister. It's fine with me." She swung to Sanford. "You with him?"

Aaron Sanford spat, brushed at his lips. "Ain't you ever going to learn, Stell? Dave's always running off at the mouth. He don't mean it. Sure I'm going—with you." He probed the bruise on his long face tenderly. "Got some interest I aim to collect from that saddle-warmer, anyway."

Stella stared at Lund. In the harsh, driving sunlight her features were rough, her eyes deep, grim pockets.

"Speak up, Dave. What's it to be? I want to know before we take another step."

Sanford shunted a glance at Lund. "He's coming along. He's come this far, he ain't fool enough to pull out now."

Stella was adamant. "Say it," she said flatly.

Dave Lund laughed. "Why, sure I'm coming, Stell. Been around you for so long now couldn't hardly get along without you. Besides, I want my cut of that thirty thousand."

"Then let's get busy," Stella said crisply. "Sooner we throw some grub in a sack and fill up the canteens, quicker we can move on."

Jim Shay moved off from the edge of the doorway. Then he dropped silently back to the kitchen.

Lifting the hook latch on the door, he stepped out onto the narrow landing, and pulled the panel shut. A shallow closet, containing brooms, mops, and cleansers, opened immediately to his right. He moved in behind it and crowded up close to the wall.

16

Now he heard the dry squeak of hinges, and in that instant realized he had made a mistake. Remnants of his hasty meal—the empty peach jar, some meat scraps and biscuit crumbs—were still on the table. He swore softly.

The door slammed. A tattoo of heels beat across the floor, the volume increasing as the outlaws and Stella neared the kitchen.

"Been somebody here," Dave Lund said.

There followed several moments of silence, and then Sanford said: "Could've been three, four days ago. Bread's dry as dust. So's the meat. Like leather."

"Was Shay, sure'n hell," Lund said. "Like as not he stopped here to swipe some grub, then lined out for Mexico."

"Mexico!" Aaron Sanford's tone was heavy with sarcasm. "Thought you was betting on him heading across the Jornada."

Lund muttered an unintelligible reply. Jim stirred uneasily. Where was Stella?

Then the girl said, "He didn't head for the border. It was him we saw riding east."

This was a flat statement, and it ended the discussion. Stella was clearly running this show.

Jars on the shelves clinked faintly. A can dropped with a loud clatter. Sanford swore. Again Stella's voice commanded.

"Look around, see if you can find a flour sack or some-

88

thing to throw this stuff in. Pillow slip will do. You know what a pillow slip is, Dave?"

Lund said, "Hell, yes, I know. What's eating you, anyway, Stell?"

"Just wanted to be sure," she murmured.

Boot heels sounded again, fading back into the interior of the house. The dipper banged against the side of the water bucket. At once Stella said, "Ought to carry extra water. Find something we can use."

"You're quite a ramrod." Aaron Sanford's voice, faintly amused, came through the wall.

"You've got the same privilege I offered Dave. If you don't like the way I do things, back out."

"Might be a damn good idea," the outlaw replied in an easy, offhanded way. "Country ain't healthy anymore. They'll have found the lard-belly's body by now."

"What if they have? It'll look like Shay's doings. Nobody knows you've been in that part of the country."

"Nobody—but Shay."

"Not much danger there. If they catch up with him he won't have time to talk—not the way that bunch of righteous Johns were feeling. And Cole's so damn slow he and that posse of his will never find him. We're the only ones who know where he went. We'll see him first, and we can quick tie up all the loose strings."

Lund returned. "Here's your pillow slip," he said. Pans on the back of the stove rattled under his heavy tread. Again there came the metallic chink of the water bucket.

Shay glanced over his shoulder. It was thirty feet to the corner of the house. If Lund or one of the others took it upon himself to step out the door and look around, he would have to move fast. The broom cabinet offered only a minimum of protection; he would be easily visible standing behind it. He waited tensely, listening to the steady gurgling of water as Lund swallowed.

"Wouldn't mind that ride so much was I sure he's toting that gold," Sanford said. "Appears to me we're just guessing on that."

"Where else could it be?" Stella asked in a sharp voice. "You claim you looked good in Garrick's cave. And you said you went through this place from top to bottom."

"Did for a fact," Lund said, moving away from the wall. "Turned it upside down. Couldn't find nothing. And we couldn't get nothing out of the old man or the old woman."

"They didn't say anything—not anything at all?"

Jim Shay, huddled against the thin plank wall, pressed even closer.

"Oh, he kept telling us we was all wrong—that he didn't have no gold around here. Kept right on saying it, even after we strung him up."

Shay shook with fury. But why the Slaussons? he thought. What connection did they have?'

"The woman—Mrs. Slausson—what did she—" Stella's tone was low, almost regretful.

"Never got around to saying much of anything. I roughed her up a mite, and then all of a sudden she just fell over. Dead when she hit the floor, I reckon."

"Proves Shay's got it then," Stella said firmly. "Garrick lied to me. Said he was sending the gold to his sister to keep for him. Only sister he had was Mrs. Slausson. Pumped that out of him one night when he was at my place. You couldn't find the gold here, so he had to be hiding it in that cave."

"And it sure wasn't there," Sanford said. "We even rooted up the floor. . . . "

"Which puts it in Shay's hands. He probably *was* in the cave when Cal died. He took the gold and lit out. That's why you couldn't find it when you came along later."

"If there was any gold to start with. . . ."

Silence dropped over the room. Jim Shay thought quickly, assembling the facts. Mrs. Slausson's brother—the one the court was seeking—was Cal Garrick. The young prospector had unwittingly signed a death warrant for the Slaussons when, in his zeal to hold Stella, he had told her his sister was keeping the gold for him.

Stella had decided on a shortcut to the riches; she had persuaded Lund and Sanford to help her get Garrick's fortune. That was why he had been shot. When the two outlaws failed to find the gold at the Slaussons', they had ridden on to the Ladrones, located the prospector, and tried to make him talk. . . .

"There's gold," Stella said, again in a patient tone. "You

think I'd've put up with that joker long as I did if I wasn't sure?"

"Could've fooled you," Lund said. "Seems he done plenty of lying about other things. Maybe he was lying all the time."

"I saw some of the nuggets. He even gave me a few. Said he always carried some around for expenses." Stella's voice became stiff. "Nobody's ever fooled me yet. No man, for sure."

"Always a first time," Sanford murmured.

"For some things. Not for me when there's a man concerned. Anyway, I wouldn't have rung you two in on this if I hadn't been sure. Could've stripped him of chicken feed myself."

"Reckon that's right," Sanford said. "About got that grub together? I'm for taking out after him soon as we can."

"All of a sudden you're in a rush," Stella observed dryly. "Made up your mind I'm right, that it?"

"Right or not, seems we ain't got much choice. We've come this far, might as well see it all the way."

Jim settled back against the wall. He knew all the answers now. But what the hell could he do about it? How could he prove what he had just heard? Before the law they would deny everything, and it would be his word against theirs— *the word of a convicted killer trying to squirm out of a life sentence in the pen.*

"You find something for water?" Stella asked.

"I'm looking," Sanford answered.

Taking them in tow would be no easy chore, Jim thought. Both men were killers, experienced in the ways of the gun-quick. And Stella could not be discounted. She was just as deadly, and likely more desperate. She was determined to recover what she felt was rightfully hers—thirty thousand dollars' worth of gold—and nothing would convince her that he didn't have it, much less that it didn't even exist. He could count on Stella going to any lengths to gain her end.

"How about a couple of these jars?" Lund suggested. "We could stow them in our saddlebags."

"Use four or five," Stella said. "And don't forget to fill the canteens."

"Yes'm," Lund said in feigned meekness.

Shay tightened. The well stood behind the house. If Lund came outside to fill the jars— He brushed at the sweat on his face, glancing again toward the corner of the house. He heard the clink of the bucket.

Through the thin boards Lund's voice said: "Enough here to do the job. Water'll be warm five minutes after we start, anyway."

"How about the canteens?" Stella reminded him.

"Fill them up when we ride out. We'll just swing around the house and stop by the pump then. No sense lugging them back and forth."

Shay relaxed. He mopped his face again. If he could move fast enough to capture all three of them, it would be only the beginning; a long fifty-mile trip to Sacramento Springs would still lie ahead. He would have his hands more than full. They would fight him every foot of the way.

He could hope for no outside help. Indeed, he must shun any riders who happened along. From what Stella had said, the Vengadors were still on the prowl: to encounter them would be fatal. They would act first and ask questions later— if ever.

Likely he would be on no better footing with George Cole and his posse. The old sheriff now thought him guilty of killing a brother lawman, and he would not be too quick to stay the guns of his posse members. Cole had already expressed his feelings when it came to a choice between spilling local blood and a stranger's.

It meant avoiding the road, keeping to the rough country lying between the river and the buttes. This wouldn't be too bad for the first few miles where there were trees and brush to shelter them from the sun; but farther on the growth petered out and nothing but desert extended the rest of the way to the settlement.

And—if he got his prisoners safely to town, what then? Would he be able to make them talk and admit their guilt? It was foolish to think so. In the end it would probably add up to one thing: they would go free, and he would have put his own neck back on the block.

He swore savagely in silence. He had no choice. He must chance it nevertheless.

He listened briefly to the dry, muffled sounds inside the house. They were getting ready to leave. Shay drew his pistol, tipped the barrel upward, and glanced at the cylinder. It was fully loaded.

He checked the yard. His sun-scorched face pulled into tight, leathery planes as tension laid its weight upon him. He stepped out from behind the cabinet.

17

Shay kicked the door wide and entered in a single long stride, his thumb drawing back the hammer of the old Colts Dragoon.

"Nobody moves!" he shouted.

Stella, her eyes wide circles, her lips parted, froze. Sanford, jaw sagging, hung motionless. Dave Lund, a quart jar of water in each hand, turned to him.

"What the hell—it's him!" he blurted.

The jars crashed to the floor, sending up twin geysers of water. The outlaw ducked to one side, clawing for his gun. Shay fired fast, aiming high. Dave Lund was no good to him dead.

The bullet caught Lund in the arm, just below the shoulder. The impact slammed him back; he staggered against the stove. His pistol, half out of the leather, thudded to the floor.

Sanford spun to fire. Shay triggered a second shot. A loud ringing sounded through the thundering echo of the Colts. Sanford's weapon twisted crazily from his grasp and went skittering into a corner of the room.

Through the dense, coiling smoke Jim saw Sanford throw himself to one side, and lunge through the doorway into the parlor. He wheeled to follow. Instantly Stella bent forward and made a grab for Lund's pistol, lying at her feet. Shay whirled to stop her. He struck her across the shoulders with his open hand, and sent her stumbling against the wall.

Snatching up Lund's pistol, he snarled, "Stay put, goddam it." He raced into the parlor. Sanford was already astride his horse and riding into the dense, feathery cover of the windbreak.

Jim swore again. A man like Aaron Sanford was always a threat, armed or not, if he was loose.

In the kitchen, Lund still sagged against the stove, his face slack with shock. He held his left arm. Blood soaked his sleeve, trickled downward, dripped off the tips of his fingers. Stella, her mouth pulled into a tight gray line, watched Jim enter with glowing hatred. She pulled herself up slowly, nursing her shoulder.

"You lousy son of a bitch," she muttered, her voice charged with venom. "I might have known. . . . It wasn't you we saw—"

"It was me," Shay said curtly.

He kicked the rear door shut and shoved a chair up against it. He was taking no chances on being rushed from behind by Sanford. One door was enough to watch. He glanced at Lund through the thinning smoke wreaths. The acrid, stinging odor of burned gunpowder still hung in the hot air.

"You're not dying," he said gruffly. "You'll live, leastwise long enough for me to get you to Sacramento Springs."

Lund straightened. "What for?"

"You know what for. You—both of you—are going to tell George Cole what this is all about—how and why you killed the Slaussons. And Rue Gilman. And Cal Garrick. I'm not paying for something you did."

"You'll play hell making me—"

"It's a long way to Sacramento Springs," Stella interrupted quietly, her self-control recovered. "You've cut yourself out quite a job, mister, if you think you can do it."

"I'll do it," Shay said. There was no sign of Sanford at the front. Jim pointed to the sack of food.

"Dump that out and make up some bandages," he told Stella. "We're getting out of here soon as you can doctor up Lund's arm."

Stella leaned against the wall, her eyes sly. "Maybe I don't feel like playing doctor, Mr. Shay."

"The hell you don't!" Jim exploded.

His strong fingers wrapped themselves about her wrist in a vise. He sent her reeling across the room and hard up against the wall. Her head struck it with a hollow sound. She sank to the floor while half a dozen cans and jars toppled and fell about her. Finally she raised her head.

"Get busy!" Shay snapped, anger rolling through him. "I'm not horsing with you. Keep remembering it's you I have to get there alive least of all."

Stella pulled herself to her feet. She picked up the sack of accumulated groceries, and dumped it onto the floor in a slow, aggravating manner. Jim looked again at the yard. If Sanford was near, he was taking pains to keep out of sight.

Dave Lund drew himself to a sitting position on the edge of the stove. He propped one foot against the woodbox and faced Jim, an odd expression in his eyes.

"Tell me, friend—you really got all that gold with you?"

Stella paused in the process of ripping the pillow slip into narrow widths. Shay shook his head.

"Never was any gold. Just a line of bull Garrick told Stella to keep her hanging around."

The girl didn't look up. "You're a liar—a damn liar," she said quietly.

Jim shrugged. "Make you feel any better, you can take a look through my saddlebags—later."

"Don't mean anything," she countered. "Like as not you've buried it somewhere."

Shay's laugh was short and harsh. "Can't make yourself believe you've been taken in—and by a big, dumb miner, can you? Garrick was suckering you all the time, lady. For once you were a bit too smart."

Stella tore at the cloth violently. "I still say you're a two-bit liar! You've got that gold—and I'll have it back before we're done."

Jim stirred. His lips parted into a crooked grin. "Suit yourself, but even if there were thirty thousand dollars' worth of it around somewhere, I don't think it would do you any good where you're going."

"Not me that's headed for the pen. . . ."

Impatience ripped through Shay. "Cut out the jawing and get on with what you're doing! I want to move out."

"Going to be rough on me, traveling," Lund protested mildly. "Why don't we hang around here for the night—"

"You'll live through it," Jim said, once again checking the yard.

Stella, still taking her time, finished tearing up the slip. Taking two of the narrow strips, she pulled back Lund's bloody shirt-sleeve and probed the wound. Lund swore softly. Stella took a bottle from the shelf and poured a liberal quantity of a strong-smelling liquid into the raw wound. Lund howled, cursing wildly. Shay, dividing his attention between them and the yard, and sweating profusely, waited impatiently for her to finish.

He wanted to get through the dense brush while it was yet daylight; it would be easier to be on the alert for Sanford. Once they reached the open desert he would not mind the darkness.

Lund was still muttering curses and moaning as Stella stood by folding one of the strips of cloth into a pad.

"You about finished?" Shay demanded.

"Pretty soon," she said slowly. "You told me to fix him up. That's what I'm doing."

She placed the pad over the wound, wasted several moments adjusting it to the proper position, then began languidly to wrap Lund's arm with another strip of cloth.

"He's fixed," Stella at last said. "Now what?"

"Take another bandage and tie his wrists together. Leave him enough room to move his fingers."

"What for?" Lund cried. "Can't do nothing with a bum arm."

"I'm making sure."

Stella complied and Shay examined the knot. It was satisfactory.

"You're next," he said to her.

She stood woodenly, not moving. Sliding the forty-four into its holster, he picked up a strip of cloth. "Over here," he snapped.

Stella sauntered toward him lazily. Then, like a cat, she lurched at him, her hand reaching for the Colts. Shay pulled her wrist away, clamping down in a crushing grip.

She cried out in pain, went to her knees, and threw her free arm about his legs. Aware that Dave Lund was closing in upon him from the left, Jim drove his knee into Stella's body, knocking her clear, and whirled, striking at Lund. The blow caught the outlaw across the face.

Anger roaring through him, Jim Shay settled back against the kitchen table. He swept the table clean in a quick, impatient gesture.

"Maybe I've got to keep you alive to do me any good," he raged. "But nothing says I can't put a couple of bullets through you. By God, you'd both better remember that!"

Stella hauled herself upright. She rubbed at her breast, her eyes accusing him. He laughed harshly.

"Don't try that on me. You've set yourself up as a man—you'll get treated as one. Get over here where I can tie you up."

She came forward slowly, her face tipped down. Lund, blood trickling from a crushed lip, leaned back against the stove. He was trembling visibly.

"You're a damn fool, Shay," he said, struggling to control his voice. "You'll never make it to the Springs with us—not with Aaron out there hanging around, just waiting for a chance to jump you."

Shay raised his eyes to the outlaw. "Maybe I'm a damn fool, but not for the reasons you think. I'll make it."

"Now, pick up that bandage," he said to Stella. "You try another stunt like that last one and you'll be the sorriest *puta* that ever rolled a drunk!"

18

Shay, watching from the window and seeing no signs of Sanford, realized he would simply have to move out with his two prisoners and take his chances. It was conceivable, of course, that Sanford would do nothing. There was little real loyalty among outlaws, and if Sanford decided it was to his best interests he would simply forget Stella and Dave Lund.

At any rate time was precious; the sun was moving relentlessly across the sky and night was not too many hours away. Many long miles lay between Slausson's and Sacramento Springs, and the only way he would ever get his prisoners there was to start.

Jim thought a bit. Then he said to Stella and Lund, "Get in the bedroom, and stand in the closet."

Lund, grumbling, moved toward the doorway. Stella hung back, saw the iron creep into Jim Shay's eyes, and hurriedly caught up with the outlaw.

"What're we doing this for?" Lund asked, halting in the opening to the storage area.

"Shut up—and get in there!" Shay barked, shoving the man through the doorway.

Then he shook his head ruefully, realizing he must control his temper. There would be a lot of this, and likely they would attempt to turn it against him as a weapon of their own. He was already on the raw edge and the trip hadn't even begun.

He closed the door to the closet and locked it, oblivious to Lund's loud protests. Stella made no sound.

He checked the rear door; it was secure. Then he stepped out onto the front landing, probing the brushy windbreak for Sanford. Seeing nothing suspicious, he crossed hurriedly to the hitchrack.

He led the horses next to the rail at the rear of the house and tethered them firmly. The coil of rope on Lund's saddle he took back into the house. Closing the front door, he dropped the crossbar into its brackets.

With Dave's and Stella's horses in the backyard, not far from where he had picketed the black, he now had but one side of the house to contend with. He shook out the rope, and opened the storage closet where Lund had been kicking persistently against the paneling.

They moved into the center of the room, Lund staring at the rope. "What's that for?"

"You," Jim replied briefly. "Turn around. Both of you."

Jim dropped a loop over Lund's shoulders and pulled it snug about the man's waist. He faulted the slipknot by taking an extra turn in the tough hemp. While the outlaw mumbled, Shay encircled Stella with the opposite end, again tying a secure knot. Then he ran the rope through his hands until he reached what he gauged to be its center, and stepped back. He looked the pair over critically.

"If either of you tries to run for it now," he said, "you won't get far. In case that isn't clear."

Lund continued muttering; Stella only nodded. Shay took up the slack in the rope. "Your horses are out back," he said. "When we get to them, take the leathers and head for the windbreak near the privy. I'll tell you when to stop. Clear?"

Stella said, "Clear," in a faint, uninterested way.

Lund shrugged. "Have yourself a ball, mister, while you got a chance. You're a damn fool if you think Aaron'll let you get away with it."

"He's the fool," Jim replied, "if he thinks he can stop me. Let's go."

He kicked the chair aside and lifted the latch. The door swung in, and Stella walked out into the bright sunshine. Lund followed a step behind her. Shay, allowing each a short length of rope, brought up the rear. Once on the stoop, he glanced again at the tamarisk while they unwound the reins to their horses, fumbling because of their bound wrists.

He brushed at the sweat on his forehead with the back of his gun hand, an unconscious gesture to relieve the tension that gripped him. Lund and Stella had released their horses.

"Across the yard," he said.

Obediently they moved out onto the hard-pack, dry and dusty from endless baking under the sun. When they were abreast of the small outhouse, Shay tugged at the rope.

"Cut right until you reach the brush. Then hold it."

At the fringe of the windbreak they stopped. Jim, paying out the rope as he went, reached the black. In the hot stillness he heard only the chirping of birds and the drone of insects. He quickly freed the gelding's reins and moved back to the yard. Sweat was now glistening on his face.

Mounted, Shay secured the rope to the fork and horn of his saddle and motioned to his prisoners. "All right, climb aboard—and keep remembering you're tied onto my horse."

Stella complied wordlessly. Lund, taking a final, futile look around the yard, his face pulled into a dark frown, put his foot into a stirrup, and hesitated.

Shay gave his end of the rope a hard jerk. "You heard me —mount up."

"All right, all right, goddamit!" the outlaw yelled, favoring his arm. "I'm doing it fast as I can."

"Better learn to move quicker than that," Shay said coldly, "unless you want me pulling your guts out."

He had expected more opposition from Stella. Either she had undergone a change of heart or she was leading him on —endeavoring to lull him into carelessness, at which point she would try something.

"Which way?" Lund's tone was hard, impatient. He had evidently expected help from Sanford by now.

"West," Jim said.

Immediately the outlaw twisted about. "West? That ain't the way to the Springs."

"Far as you're concerned it is," Jim snarled. "I expect that *compadre* of yours is waiting somewhere along the main road for a chance to jump me. I don't aim to accommodate him. That what's bothering you?"

"How the hell would I know where he is?"

"You don't, any more than I do. But that's my guess. And he's holding off until dark. He's got no guts to try me without a gun in his hand so he needs a little something to even up the odds—darkness.

"Right now I expect he's sittting up there waiting for us to come riding by—only we won't. We're taking the desert."

Lund's eyes opened. Even Stella lifted her head. The outlaw gasped, "For Christ's sake—you don't mean that?"

"That's the way we're going. Pull out. More we cover tonight, the less we'll have tomorrow. I'll tell you when to turn north."

Lund shrugged helplessly. "You're loco, Shay," he moaned. "Plumb loco."

They led off into the brush and trees. The heat had diminished a little, although the afternoon was getting on. There was a different sort of heat in the valley. Here where there was green, rank growth—primroses, thick bushes, Osage orange and cottonwood trees, flowers and deep grass—there was also moisture, a heavy, uncomfortable humidity. On the plains, as on the deserts, the heat was dry and penetrating. It drilled deep into a man, but there was a cleanness to it. If he had to make a choice, Jim thought as they moved on into the lowering sun, he would take the desert.

He grinned at himself mopping at the sweat on his face. Then he jerked himself about on the saddle roughly and rubbed at his neck, striving to organize his waning senses, retain a degree of alertness. He could not afford to lower his guard for a moment. Sanford could still be close by, simply holding back in the shadows, waiting for his chance. Sanford probably wouldn't forsake his friends; he still didn't know there was no thirty thousand dollars in gold.

They pushed on at a monotonous pace, Shay rocking ceaselessly back and forth with the rhythmic step of the black. A rabbit scooted out from under the hooves of Lund's horse, setting up a loud rattle of dry leaves as it raced away. Shay came bolt upright, his gun springing into his hand, and then settled back. He swore under his breath, but the cottontail had done him a favor; it had roused him from the near stupor of his fatigue.

He glanced about. Fifteen feet or so away from him Dave

Lund rode. The loop about his waist appeared snug. Shay kept Stella at a similar distance.

The two rode side by side, scarcely more than an arm's length separating them. Shay would have preferred them farther apart, but the dense undergrowth made this impractical. When they reached the desert he would split them wide.

The sun finally slipped behind the bluffs, leaving a brilliant spray of rose, purple, and yellow in its wake. Shay, doggedly fighting drowsiness, kept focusing his smarting eyes on his prisoners.

Dave Lund was looking back over his shoulder now, a hard grin on his lips. Dave was clearly watching his chances shape up.

"Turn around—goddam you!" Shay yelled. "I catch you grinning at me again, I'll put a sack over your head."

Lund laughed, and faced forward. He leaned sideways and whispered something to Stella. She nodded.

Jim removed his hat, rubbed his fingers through his hair, and scratched at his scalp. He mopped his face, stretched, and took a swallow from his canteen, noting absently that it was somewhat less than half full.

The import of that struck him suddenly—it was all the water he had. Busy securing his prisoners at Slausson's, he had forgotten to refill the container. The old molasses jug swinging from his saddle was empty too. Stella and Lund might also be crucially low on water; they had been getting it when he had moved in on them.

There was no water along the desert. The nearest was the Rio Grande, miles to the east—and he could not risk going there. He cursed himself softly, and hoped that Lund and Stella had at least a little water.

He raised his eyes to the darkening sky. The ragged red-brown line of bluffs lay just ahead. The course he had followed had taken them away from the centuries-old highway that connected Mexico City with Santa Fe and all in-between points, and now lay far behind. The vast, paralleling desert that extended almost to the outskirts of the settlement was not far now—just where the bluffs sloped down to melt into the desolate plain. Shay breathed easier.

"Swing north," he called. "And no tricks. . . . I'm watching you close."

But for how long, he wondered.

19

Jim Shay fought his faltering senses to a state of near alertness. The sun had vanished an hour ago. Stars were out, assisting the moon, and the brush, scrubby trees, and now more prevalent rocks as well as the sand lay bathed in a cool silver glow.

The dark figures of Dave Lund and Stella were silhouetted against the night a dozen paces ahead. He could dimly see the loops around their waists. Their horses plodded dully on, heads low, heedless of the brush whipping at their legs, a mute indication of their worn condition.

The black was little better off. He would be forced to call a halt soon. He had hoped this could wait until they were in the open, beyond the black shadows of the underbrush, but there was a limit to the endurance of horseflesh, and of men.

Somewhere off to the left in a pocket of scrub oak something moved, setting up a dry rattle. Shay's hand dropped to the pistol at his hip. Aaron Sanford could be out there—about to make his try. Jim drew his weapon. The pistol he had taken from Lund rested inside his belt.

They rode on, tense—waiting, listening. The noise did not erupt again. Probably another rabbit, or some larger animal. Still, it could have been Sanford. Up ahead Dave Lund chuckled softly.

"Laugh, you bastard!" Jim muttered bitterly. "Tomorrow it'll be my turn."

Tomorrow. . . .

If he managed to hang onto Stella and Lund, hold off Sanford, get by the posses, survive the desert, and reach Sacramento Springs with almost no water and horses barely able to walk—then there would be a tomorrow.

He raised himself in the stirrups, easing the dull ache in his muscles. He could not see the broadly spreading desert yet. The brush was thinning, though, and the row of bluffs to the west was almost invisible.

The heat had broken finally and it was cool. He fought against sleep as a man fights against a deadly enemy. He watched Stella turn about, pull and tug at her blanket roll, take from it a light buckskin jacket. She could not put it on because of her linked wrists, but she draped it over her shoulders.

Lund sat well forward on his horse, chin sunk into his chest, undoubtedly sleeping. Jim must stay awake—he dared not close his eyes—though Lund dozed to his heart's satisfaction. And when a moment of emergency presented itself, Lund would be fresh, rested, and wholly awake, while Shay could only hope to be sufficiently alert to meet the test.

Now the desert appeared through the screening brush, a glowing world of deceptive peacefulness and beauty. Jim sighed gratefully—and then a dark shape was hurtling through the night toward him.

He caught the brief, brittle flash of a knife blade in the pale light, heard a yell—Aaron Sanford's voice—and jerked himself to one side. But the outlaw, crouched on a large boulder and all but hidden by foliage, was too close. Shay felt the solid smash of Sanford's weight against him.

They fell from the startled black, the outlaw clawing for Jim's throat. Again he saw the glitter of starlight on the knife blade. He reached out frantically, groping, and gripped the outlaw's wrist. They struck the ground, Shay flat on his back. Breath gushed from him and a shower of tiny lights exploded before his eyes.

Instinct held his fingers locked about Sanford's wrist, and with his free arm he knocked aside the clutching hand at his throat. He jerked free and rolled to the side. A few yards away he could see the black, rearing and shying as he tried to get clear of the rope dragging at his saddle.

Farther over Lund was shouting curses, evidently still

unable to get free of the rope that encircled him because of the tension placed on it from the excited gelding. He could not see Stella.

As he leaped to his feet, Sanford closed with him, slashing wickedly with the knife. The outlaw's face was streaked with dirt. His eyes were narrowed, his mouth hung open as he gulped for air. Cornered against the brush, Shay reached for his gun. He fired quickly—too quickly.

Unharmed, Sanford lunged. Jim hurled himself to the left, tripped, and went down. Sanford fell across him, pinning his legs. He slashed with his knife. Shay, silently desperate now for his life, clubbed at the outlaw's head with the heavy Colts. He heard the barrel strike. Sanford cursed and rolled to one side. Blood was suddenly streaming down his face, mingling with the dirt and sweat.

The outlaw pulled back, hung for a moment half upright, then staggered to his feet. He was still dazed. Shay, his breath coming in great, painful gasps, crawled into the brush, got to his feet, and whirled. Sanford had turned, too. He shook his head and moved in again.

Metal glittered on the ground between them. Lund's pistol had fallen from Shay's belt during the struggle. Both men leaped for it. A fraction nearer, Shay kicked out. His toe struck the weapon and sent it hurtling off into the darkness.

Now Sanford was on him. Instinctively he struck out, strength coming from some previously untapped source within him. The blow staggered the outlaw, but he stayed on his feet. He was clawing blindly. He seized Jim by the arm and whirled him off-balance.

Shay went over backward; the shock of earth jarred him solidly. He had an instant's glimpse of Sanford's distorted face, teeth bared, as he surged in, knife poised and still glittering in the pale light. Shay fired. He fired again. Sanford jerked away, as though seized by some mighty hand. He went to one knee, regained his footing and plunged off into the brush like a wounded animal.

Jim, sucking deep for air to fill his throbbing lungs, pulled himself upright. His legs were trembling and his knees threatened to buckle, but he made it to the fringe of underbrush. He could not see Sanford, but he could hear the outlaw rushing away, crashing through the dry growth. Then came a moment of quiet. And after that the quick beat of a horse trotting off into the night.

Shay leaned against the boulder. He still had Lund and Stella. He sank back, his head swimming. He was having difficulty regaining his breath, and his legs still shook. He became aware of a stinging along his rib cage, just below the left armpit. Exploring it with his fingers, he felt the thick stickiness of blood. Sanford had almost succeeded.

He lifted his head to stare fixedly in front of him. He saw the gelding first, standing quietly in a pool of moonlight. The big horse appeared exhausted.

Jim heaved upright, and approached him with slow, uncertain steps. The rope, still taut, stretched off into the brush. Gun in hand, Shay followed it out to its end. Dave Lund lay on the ground. The crazed black had moved too fast for him. He had been jerked off his feet and dragged into the tough, unyielding trunk of a squat juniper. The outlaw was stunned, but that was all.

Stella. . . .

Jim wheeled. He traced the other line and found Stella, gasping for breath, slumped forward on her saddle. She was fumbling weakly with the knot in the riata, endeavoring to loosen its choking grasp about her waist.

Shay brushed away her hands and pulled slack into the rope. She sagged lower, retching as she struggled for breath. After a few moments she stared dumbly at him.

The look in her eyes sent a sudden, unreasonable anger soaring through him. "You asked for it!" he shouted.

Lund had recovered himself by now and was sitting up, rubbing his head ruefully.

"On your feet," Shay snapped, dragging him to an upright position. "And mount up!"

Lund sagged toward his bay, to cling to the horn. "Hell— I can't ride—"

"You goddam well will—either on the saddle or across it. Makes no difference to me."

"Arm of mine's killing me," Lund moaned. "That damned horse—"

"I'm bleeding for you," Shay said coldly. "What's it going to be?"

"Can't we rest here a spell?"

"So's Sanford can take another crack at me—that what you're thinking? Forget it. He's hit—maybe bad, and I doubt if he'll be coming back—but I'm not fool enough to chance it. Get on that horse!"

Lund turned to the bay, his movements aggravatingly slow. Shay, anger a wild force in him now, seized Lund under the arms and boosted him roughly onto the saddle. He settled himself on his black; immediately an overwhelming wave of exhaustion claimed him, leaving him without the will to go on.

He sat quiet for a full minute. Then, rousing, he put the gelding into motion. Ahead, Dave Lund had brought his horse up alongside Stella's, clearing the rope of entangling brush as he went. The worn cavalcade moved forward again slowly.

Shay forced his wavering attention to their back trail, to the dark islands of brush and shadows on either side. He did not think it likely Sanford would try again: the outlaw had been close when the bullet struck and there was a good possibility the second shot had driven into him. But Aaron Sanford was a man Jim did not know well, and he couldn't predict his next step. He might make a second attempt.

A quarter of an hour later they broke into the open. The land flowed away before them in pale, glowing contours, soft as summer clouds, seemingly having no end to the west, to the north, or the east. Shay, barely conscious, felt a stir of relief, and his sagging, depleted spirits lifted slightly. Now they could rest.

He continued on, however, until a good piece of ground separated them from the brush. Lund and the girl came off their horses slowly and sank to the sand, sprawling out full-length on the still warm earth.

Still connected to them by the rope, Jim Shay followed suit, taking care to place himself so as to keep an eye on his prisoners and also watch the dark wall of brush to the south. He could not get Sanford out of his mind.

He'd finish it, he vowed now, and he grinned into the night, a defiant grimace. He'd made it this far in spite of all hell; he'd make it the rest of the way.

He allowed a full hour to pass, and then pulled himself to

his feet. He took a small sip from his canteen to ease his dry throat, then yelled at Lund and Stella to mount up. They struggled to standing positions. Lund reached for his canteen, found it empty, and hurled it to the ground.

Wordlessly Stella passed her container to the outlaw. The girl had a small drink too, and again slung the canteen across the horn of her saddle. She had a little water left, Jim saw; he prayed there would be enough.

They moved on, the horses plodding heavily across the soft, gradually cooling sand. Rabbits skittered from under their hooves now and then, but they drew little attention from the weary beasts other than a flick of the ears. Coyotes barked inquisitively from respectable distances. Once an owl hooted, questioning their sluggish passage.

As the night wore on their stops for rest grew more frequent. There were no signs of Aaron Sanford trailing them across the silent reaches, and Jim allowed himself the luxury of thinking that the outlaw had called it off.

Lund, apparently disheartened by Sanford's failure to deliver him, rode head down, shoulders slumped, far from his usual sardonic self. And Stella, still withdrawn and coldly remote, made no comments.

With the first streaks of gray showing in the east a wind sprang up, stirring the dust and quickly covering the land with a thin tan haze. But that, too, passed, and shortly thereafter the sun rose.

20

It was abruptly hot.

The flaming salmon streaks, which replaced the pearl-gray above the Capitans and the Oscuras to the east, had scarcely fused into the blue of the sky when the sun began its brutal, devastating work again.

It found them in a wild, broken country some fifteen miles to the south and west of the settlement—a savage area of narrow ravines, rock-ribbed arroyos, thin, thorned brush and cholla cactus. This was a tortured, lonely world, claimed only by the scorpions, rattlesnakes, and velvet ants.

Jim Shay and his two companions were dust-covered, soaked with sweat. Their skins were dry, burned black and leathery by the fierce sun and scrubbed to a bark-like roughness by the raw winds. Their lips were cracked, and a gray rime encircled their mouths and lined the pockets of their swollen, blood-shot eyes.

They still rode in triangular formation—a grotesque driver commanding a grotesque team.

The horses staggered now as they walked over the heated sand, their bent heads and trembling legs mute demands for water and rest. When an hour had passed and the party had made only negligible progress, Shay tugged at the ropes to signal for a halt.

Lund and Stella pulled in and waited for Shay to move up. The gelding was too worn to take the extra steps. Shay crawled from the saddle and dropped to the ground. He

110

stayed there for a time, his knees bent, his weight slung against the horse, his head resting on his arm, as he closed his eyes to shut out the merciless ball above.

Lund and the girl dismounted. They simply stood then, motionless in the small block of shade afforded by the horses' bodies. Lund looked back at Shay.

"We ain't going to make it," he said tonelessly. "Twelve, fifteen son of a bitching miles—and we won't make it. We're dying right here."

Shay, a gaunt, haggard ghost of a man stared back stonily. "We'll make it," he said. "I'm not letting you die . . . either one of you. I'm taking you to the Springs."

"Fifteen miles . . . " the outlaw muttered. "Might as well be fifteen hundred. . . ."

"We'll make it."

It was a matter of pride now, too, of hard-core will and bullheaded determination, along with the need to clear his name. All the other issues had somehow gotten lost during the last endless, agonizing hours.

He thought only of reaching the settlement alive with his two prisoners. He had to beat them, and he had to beat the desert—as he had beaten the Jornada and Aaron Sanford.

"We'll make it!" he said for the third time, in a cracked voice.

They rested for a quarter of an hour, then mounted and hammered their reluctant horses into motion once more. The sun lifted higher, and the scattered heat-blasted cacti, starving mesquite, and creosote bushes appeared to wither before their eyes. Lizards panted in the meager, infrequent lattices of shade beneath the sparse growth, and from the half-exposed crevice of a rock ledge a rattler buzzed a threat in vain.

They rode for a mile at a time now, resting briefly and riding on yet again. Near midmorning Jim gave the last of their water to the horses, pouring it onto a piece of cloth and squeezing it dry in turn into the throats of the suffering brutes. They each turned wild at the taste of the few drops, but he managed to calm them somewhat by swabbing their lips and nostrils with the moist cloth.

Exhausted by his simple chore, Jim leaned once again on the gelding, and stared out over the glittering flats to the north. Ten miles at most, he reckoned. It seemed as distant as the earth's poles.

Lund, his scorched face slack under its coat of sweat and dust, watched Shay with dull eyes.

"You're putting us through hell for nothing," he mouthed. "Reckon you know that."

"We'll see," Jim mumbled.

"Even was you to get us there, which I'm doubting, you've got nothing on us you can prove. . . . All you've got is what you heard us say—and that sure as hell ain't proof. . . . Forget it, Shay. Take this goddamed rope off us, turn us loose. Then maybe we can make it."

Shay drew the old Dragoon, the gesture more instinctive than necessary. "We're getting there," he said with sullen patience.

Lund produced a harsh grin. "Maybe *we* will, but I got doubts about you. You're ready to cave in right now. Stella and me have still got a couple hours left in us."

They did have the edge on him. . . . He had been going since Monday. And this—he fumbled, struggled to channel his thoughts—this was Thursday. . . . No, it was Friday—Friday morning. Four nights and four days. . . . He had scarcely been off the saddle in all that time. He had crossed and recrossed the searing Jornada—and now he was bucking this blistered, sweltering killer called the *Recreo del Diablo*—the playground of the devil.

Leaden weights dragged at him. There would be trouble now too. That bastard Lund had tipped his hand. As they drew nearer the settlement he would make his move. Jim would have to be more alert now than ever, exactly when it would be hardest.

He settled his wavering gaze on Stella. She would make her try, too. That was as he had suspected; in her mind, all the way, there had been a plan. The pair were scheming together. Well, let them. . . . Damn them both to hell. . . . He still had the gun. . . . He was still running the show. . . .

Far to the east a boil of dust took shape against the horizon, drifting lazily southward. Shay watched it with slack disinterest. It would take a number of horses to kick up so much dust. Maybe it was one of the posses—or it could be the stagecoach bound for El Paso. It didn't matter. The distance was so great that their own small dust would pass unnoticed. And even if it were observed and the riders turned out to be men searching for him, they still wouldn't be able to catch up with him before he reached the Springs with his prisoners. If he kept going, if he didn't falter and go down.

He pulled himself with great effort onto the black and sank into the bow of his saddle. "I'm more dead than alive," he muttered, half aloud, and urged the black forward. Stella and the outlaw had made no move to mount.

"Let's go," he said, his voice a croak.

"Stell and me—we're deciding whether we want to or not," Lund said. His tone was vaguely questioning.

He was challenging, testing, seeing how far he could go. Jim drew his pistol. His arm quivered as he took aim. He squeezed off a shot. The bullet spurted sand over Lund's feet. The outlaw flinched, glared back angrily.

"Next time I'll raise my sights some," Shay said. Lund climbed onto his bay. Stella was studying Shay quietly, her eyes drawn to narrow slits, her lips a thin, colorless line. After a moment she got onto her saddle.

Shay holstered the Colt's, and they moved on. Ride, rest, ride. . . . Finally, in the late morning, the sun blasting them near the height of its merciless fury, they were forced to walk the horses. The blistering sand burned through the soles of their boots, drilled upward into their legs. Its steel lances stabbed into their bodies, sapped them steadily of their remaining strength.

Shay staggered uncertainly, supporting himself by clinging to the black, allowing the horse half to drag, half to pull him along. Unholy fires raged in his throat. Dave Lund's challenge was the only force that kept him going.

Then he saw smoke in the sky ahead. . . That *had* to be the settlement. But how far? Two miles? If he could just stay on his feet a little longer . . . another hour. . . .

He pushed on, driving himself mercilessly, barely guarding the two ahead of him. Lund's bay came to a halt, front legs spraddled, head so low his nose was only inches from the broiling sand. The beast's sides were heaving, and his eyes bulged as though coming free of their sockets. He began to sink slowly. Lund turned to Shay.

"He's done for. . . ."

"Keep walking," Shay said in a wooden, emotionless voice. "Keep on walking. . . ."

Lund turned wordlessly, and staggering slightly, moved to Stella's mount. He threw out his good arm, grasping the cantle of her saddle to support himself. And they continued.

Shay looked upward, silently cursed the glowing sun, its sweltering shafts, the endless, glittering miles. He lowered his head. Abruptly his pulses quickened.

Ahead the desert seemed to fall away. For a few paces he saw only the horizon, and then, as Stella and Dave Lund came to a stop and he moved up to them, he looked down into the narrow valley that lay between the river and the hills. Sprawled out only a mile distant lay Sacramento Springs, it tin roofs shining in the hot sunlight.

A hard grin crossed his lean, dark face. He winced as a new crack split his lip—but that didn't matter now. He sagged against the worn gelding.

"We made it," he said in a hoarse voice. "By God—we made it!"

Stella wheeled to him slowly. Her face was a stiff, dust-streaked patchwork of lines. The strip of cloth that had bound her wrists together now dangled from one arm, rotted away from sweat and exertion. In her hand she held a small nickeled revolver. It glinted brightly in the streaming rays.

"*We* made it," she said. "You didn't."

21

In the heated, shimmering hush that followed, only the
painful breathing of the horses and the dry clack of insects
in the stubby weeds could be heard. Farther down the slope
a red-brown hawk skimmed the rocks on pointed wings,
the band across his tail flashing white as he veered sharply
back and forth in search of prey.

Dave Lund found his voice. "By God, Stell—ain't you the
cute one! Why didn't you dig out that damned iron sooner?"

Stella watched Shay with a steady, murderous intensity.
"Would have—if I'd got the chance."

"Chance? Back there on the desert, in the dark—"

"Too late then. I'd have been a fool to kill him. We needed
him to get us across. Never have made it, otherwise."

"Well, we sure'n hell don't need him now," Lund said,
tugging at the rope around his waist. He paused, to stare at
Stella. "Go ahead—shoot. What're you holding back for?"

"The gold," she said. "He's got it hid somewhere. Ought
to be a way of making him talk. . . ."

Shay's mind was functioning sluggishly, only half taking
in her words. "Gold," he said thickly. "Told you before.
There's no gold. Garrick lied."

Stella never removed her flat-surfaced eyes from him.
"Look in his saddlebags, Dave. Ought to be some of it there.
He wouldn't cache it all."

Lund, finally free of the lariat, moved to the gelding. He
came in from the side opposite Jim. His wrists still loosely

115

bound, the outlaw fiddled with the buckles of the pouches, laid back the flap, and began to empty the contents onto the ground.

"Nothing here," he said.

"There's two of them!" Stella said impatiently.

Stella was only a little better off than he, Jim saw. Her face was drawn. She stood with her feet planted far apart, bracing herself, and the hand that gripped the small-caliber revolver trembled. She was not far from collapse.

Lund moved in from the rump of the gelding, hazing the horse roughly into swinging around. He went through the second saddlebag, again dumping Jim's belongings onto the sand.

"Nothing here, either," he announced gloomily. "Maybe he's telling us straight. Maybe Garrick was stringing you along."

Shay, head bent forward in absolute fatigue, waited in the broad sunlight. He felt a wave of giddiness pass through him. He shook himself. The damn heat. The damned heat. He called on his reserves, fought to clear his mind.

"Never was any gold," he said doggedly. "You did your killing for nothing."

Stella's jaw hardened. "There was," she said unreasoningly. "Thirty thousand dollars' worth. Maybe you didn't get it— and maybe you did."

"You think I'd put myself through this hell if I had it?" Shay demanded warily. "Use some sense. By this time I'd have been in Mexico, enjoying myself, not standing out here in this sun, cooking."

"He ain't got it, Stell," Lund said, convinced. "Like as not it's still back there in the Ladrones. It ain't in that cave, but there's a lot of other places on the slopes where Garrick could've hid it."

"It's somewhere," she said dully. "We've got to find it."

Lund looked off toward the settlement. "Maybe we better not use that gun," he said. "Some sodbuster just might hear it."

"What'll we do with him, then?"

"No problem. I'll tie him up, leave him laying here on the sand. Shape he's in the sun'll take care of him quick."

Lund circled the black. Taking care not to place himself between Shay and Stella's revolver, he backed up to her.

"Knife in my pocket. Fish it out and cut these here rags off my wrists."

With her free hand Stella drew the jackknife. She opened the blade with her teeth and severed the rotting cloth strip. Lund chaffed the skin of his injured arm briskly. Then he made his way to the mound of articles removed from the saddlebags and selected several lengths of rawhide.

"These'll do fine," he said. "Rawhide'll hold him till hell freezes over—only hell don't freeze over in this Godforsaken country."

Shay braced himself. They had not disarmed him yet. The Colts still hung at his side.

"Stand still!" Stella's voice was a sharp whip. "Take that gun away from him, Dave."

The outlaw stepped in behind him and he felt the lessening of weight at his hip as the old Dragoon was lifted from its leather. He threw off the helplessness that gripped him then. He must think of some alternate plan.

Lund held the cords in one hand. A triumphant grin cracked his mouth.

"Going to be real pleasured by this," he said. "Hold out your paws—"

Shay hesitated for a second, then began slowly to raise his hands, his lethargy only a pose now. With effort he extended his arms, and then, with a sudden movement, he reached out and clamped his fingers hard around the wound in Dave Lund's biceps. The outlaw screamed with pain. Jim spun him about and flung him straight at Stella.

She fired twice in rapid succession, the little pistol making an odd, dry, splatting sound. Then Lund stumbled into her and she went down. Shay, scooping up his own weapon where the outlaw had dropped it, staggered forward. Stella's nickeled revolver glittered in the sand. With an oath he kicked it off the rim of the slope into a welter of loose rocks below.

Standing back, weaving uncertainly, sweat pouring off him, Shay glared down at Stella and the groaning Lund.

"On your feet!" he gasped, his voice grating and ungoverned.

They struggled upright. A burned patch smoldered slowly in

Lund's shirt-sleeve where one of Stella's bullets had made a near miss. Cursing, the outlaw pinched out the fire.

"Get the rope," Shay ordered tautly. "Put it back on."

The outlaw, nursing his wound, now bleeding again, and reeling slightly, moved to the end of the riata and picked it up. He placed it about his waist and secured it.

"Tighter," Shay said in the same new wild tone.

Lund groaned, but pulled the rope closer. Shay reached for his end and gave it a hard jerk. The oulaw went to his knees. A yell of pain burst from his lips as he unthinkingly threw out both arms, trying to keep from falling full-length.

"Goddam you, Shay—"

Jim yanked on the rope again. "Start down that slope," he snapped. "You fall again, I'll let the black drag you the rest of the way to town."

Stella was forcing herself to speak. He could see it in her tired eyes.

"I've—I've made a mistake," she said heavily. "Had you figured all wrong. Can't—can't we straighten this out without going to the sheriff?"

"You're a little late with that," Shay said. "Get moving."

"Shut up, damn you!" Lund yelled suddenly. "Was you that had this all figured out. You put us up to doing it. . . . Partners you said we were—partners in thirty thousand dollars' worth of—"

Jim threw his weight against the rope. Lund, off-balance, went down again onto the scorching sand. Stella, jerked to one side, caught herself.

"Move—damn you both!" Shay shouted, once more fighting off the gray haze that threatened to close in on him.

They started down the grade, slipping and sliding on the loose shale. They reached the bottom, and struck out across a field of knee-high alfalfa. It was a little cooler as they made their slow way through the sweet, green-blossomed hay. Ahead, Shay saw the glint of water. The black caught the smell of it, and surged forward eagerly. It was a small irrigation ditch, running full. Stumbling, half running, Jim and the others reached it together, and plunged recklessly into its silty depth.

Shay, on his knees, water purling about the lower half of his body, sloshed the cooling fluid against his face, down his neck and chest, gulping huge mouthfuls, oblivious to the sand and soil in it. Then he sat back on his heels, reveling in the freshness of the moment. Above him, glum and silent, Stella and Dave Lund were still splashing themselves, while below the horses drank noisily.

A quarter of an hour later they resumed their march to the settlement, now only a few hundred yards distant. The deadening weight of near-exhaustion still hung, like a gigantic millstone, about Shay's shoulders.

A man working an adjoining field paused at his labors, leaned upon his hoe, and stared at them curiously from the distance. Jim coiled the rope and moved up to walk between Stella and the outlaw, allowing the horses to trail behind. To an onlooker they would now appear to be only three rather dusty persons, worn and sun-baked, walking into town.

Nevertheless, Jim took no risks. He kept to the fields as long as he could, then entered the scatter of houses by little-used side lanes. They reached the alley that lay behind the jail and turned into it. Stella stopped abruptly.

She was the old Stella again, hard, tough, and insolent. Particles of sand still clung to her hair and thick brows.

"I'm warning you, Shay—this is your last chance."

"Warning me?" Jim repeated with a faded smile. "Seems you've got it twisted around."

"No. . . . You're forgetting how things stand. You're walking into your own trap. It's you they're looking for, not me . . . or Dave."

"Aim to change that. Once I'm through talking to Cole, he'll—"

"He'll what? What makes you think Cole will believe what you say?"

Shay hesitated. "He's got to believe it. . . ."

He was immune to the weariness by now, a wooden man capable only of automatic motion. It seemed months since he had slept, eaten a square meal, enjoyed a cup of coffee or a drink of whiskey. But it was about finished now—one way or another. And there was more truth than he liked to think in Stella's words.

They came to the jail. Around them Sacramento Springs lay in midday heat, silent except for the cicadas in the trees and the meadowlarks whistling from the fields. Jim draped the reins of the gelding over a roughhewn bar. He waited while Stella anchored her mount, and then all three moved to the rear door.

Praying that it would be unlocked so he would not have to take his prisoners around to the front, he tested the knob. The panel swung inward.

Gun in hand, he motioned for Lund and the girl to enter. He was already shaping up in his mind the things he would say to George Cole. He stepped in behind the pair, the coiled lariat still looped over his shoulder. They walked down the corridor, past the empty cells, and into the lawman's quarters.

The office was deserted.

22

Jim stood for a long minute in the center of the stuffy room, shoulders down, physical and mental exhaustion a tremendous, crushing force on him. He had gambled on Cole, or at least Miguel Sierra, being there. Even then he would have been on treacherous ground—now the danger was multiplied tenfold. Without the protection of the law, he could become a quick and handy victim of the Vengadors, or any lynch party still convinced that he had murdered the Slaussons . . . and Rue Gilman.

"Got your foot in it this time for sure, mister," Dave Lund said. "Smart thing for you to do is turn us loose—then get the hell out of here. We won't give you away. Just head out the back and keep riding."

Head out the back—keep riding. . . .

It would be easy—and maybe it was smart advice. They had been seen by people when they entered the settlement. Possibly a few would have recognized him. And there was always quick word of mouth in these towns.

"Wasting your time, anyway. You won't convince the law you're innocent. Or that we had anything to do with the Slaussons, either. You ain't got any proof, Shay. . . . None. . . . And you've already been convicted by a jury. You're bucking a stacked deck."

"I did not kill the Slaussons," Shay said slowly. "Or the deputy—or Cal Garrick, either, if they're thinking that. You

121

damn well know it. Was you and Sanford all the way. And
I'm going to prove it."

"You won't get a chance to. They won't bother to take you
to the pen now. Like as not they'll hang you right here in the
street for Gilman's murder. . . . Sure don't pay to blast a
lawman."

Stella spoke. "I'm well known around here too, you know.
You'll have a hard time proving anything like murder on
me. Happens I've got a few friends—good friends who won't
like seeing me in trouble."

Shay wiped at the sweat on his face for a long moment.

"Guess you know all I've got to do is step out that door,
holler right loud a couple of times, and you'll have a lynching party coming for you quick," Lund said. "Not a man in
the county wouldn't jump at the chance to put a noose around
your neck for what you've done. . . ."

"For what you've done," Shay corrected coldly.

"All right—for what we've done, but you're the man they
figure to collect from. Come on, Shay, put away that gun
and get this rope off us."

Out in the street, in the direction of Cook's, they could
hear voices now. Jim must decide—and quick. The voices
could have something to do with his being there. He looked at
Lund and the girl. He had a swift image of what he had found
at the Slausson farm that Sunday—the woman crumpled on
the floor, dead, her husband hanging like a limp, battered
dummy from the ceiling of the family parlor. He remembered
how Rue Gilman had buckled, clutching at his chest, and
while that did not diminish his dislike for the deputy, he
felt again the sickening shock of watching ruthless murder.
. . . And Cal Garrick, his life bubbling away through a
ragged hole in his breast; all because of a lie, and gold that
didn't exist.

It would be a one-way road if he ducked and ran, a trail
that never ended. And it could be a one-way road if he did not.
But a man had to live with himself. Maybe he wouldn't
stay alive long enough to regret it—as Jim Shay saw it, he had
only one choice.

He straightened, his jaw set, his tired eyes rock-hard. "Into
those cells—both of you," he snapped. "And quick about it!"

If a delegation of the town's citizens was on the way at

least he'd then have his prisoners where he could handle them.

Lund stared at him. "What the hell—"

"You heard me. I'm locking you up until Cole gets here."

Lund swore wildly. "If I didn't know better, I'd say you're drunk. But I know better, so you must be plumb crazy! We're giving you a chance to get out of this. Ain't you got sense enough to grab it?"

Shay caught the outlaw by the shoulder and shoved him toward the corridor. Lund stumbled, collided with the wall, and broke into a fresh round of oaths.

Shay glared back at Stella. "What are you stalling for?"

She gave him one furious look, and darted for the door. "You're not locking me up! I'll yell—"

Jim seized the rope peeling off the coil slung over his arm. He trapped it and pulled hard. Stella, checked off-balance in mid-step, slammed up against Cole's desk and crumpled to the floor. She lay there, gasping. Then her mouth drew into an ugly line.

"Just like all the others. Tough—when it comes to a woman."

"You're no woman," Shay said. "You're a greedy bitch. Now get back to that cell."

He shoved Lund deeper into the hallway. Stella followed, trembling with rage.

Shay left the rope about their waists, placed them in separate cells, and locked the gratings. With slow, heavy steps, he made for the rear door, slid the bolt, and returned to the office. He wanted to have only the front entrance to worry about. He settled down on one of the straight-backed chairs. Immediately he rose. His eyes were so leaden he dare not relax, get the least bit comfortable. To fall asleep would be openly inviting disaster.

He began to pace back and forth in the stifling room. Each step was a terrible effort.

He could still hear voices coming from the street, but he was not inclined to risk stepping outside the door. If anyone did move on the jail, he was ready to greet them with a full measure of trouble, of his own making.

He found himself dozing as he walked. He helped himself to a drink of water and then poured a dipperful over his head. The water wasn't cold but it was wet, and that wakened him to some extent. He resumed his wooden, monotonous march.

Dave Lund began to abuse him from the confines of his cell, alternately cursing him with a fluency accrued from a life of close association with trail saloons and border bordellos, and pleading with him to be smart, to use his head and run for it while there was yet time—after unlocking the cells.

His words struck Jim and fell off, lost.

Shadows crossed the barred window adjacent to the door. The soft *tunk-a-tunk* of weary horses walking in the dust and the rising volume of voices roused Shay. He faced the jail's entrance. Through the open door he could now see George Cole, trail-worn and dusty, accompanied by a half a dozen or so riders, pulling to a stop at the hitchrack. A considerable crowd clustered about them.

"See anything of him?" a voice called.

"What about the Veng—the other boys?" another asked. "Maybe they got him. . . ."

George Cole swung stiffly from his saddle. He settled himself on the ground, a man too old for such work. He rubbed at his crotch, relieving the taut muscles of his thighs.

"Naw—nobody seen him," he said with a long, drawn-out sigh.

He turned his attention to the members of his posse. "Obliged, men," he said, and started for the door. Miguel Sierra, evidently waiting somewhere in front of the jail, stalked in behind the sheriff.

Jim drew back into the corner. Lund had fallen silent, and now there sounded only murmurings in the street, and the dry clacking of an alarm clock on a shelf above the safe.

Cole walked into the heat-trapped room. He came up short immediately when he saw Shay.

"For the love of God!" he said. "I'm out combing the damned country for him—and he's standing right here in my own office."

23

Shay, a lean, haggard, hollow-eyed scarecrow, staggered forward. He sagged against a corner of the desk, supporting himself with his arms. Sheer determination kept him on his feet.

"Got the real killers locked in your cells."

His voice was a hoarse rasp, and the words were thick; they came out as though dragged forcibly across his cracked, scabbed lips by some unseen power.

Cole continued to stare at him. "The real killers?"

"Two of them, anyway. . . . Third one—name of Sanford—jumped me on the yonder side of the desert. I shot him. Could be dead."

"Killers of who?" the lawman pressed quietly.

"The Slaussons. And Rue Gilman—and a prospector named Garrick."

"He's lying!" Dave Lund shouted from the rear of the jail. "He's lying to save his own goddam hide. Let me out of here, Sheriff. That bastard's gone loco."

Cole motioned to Sierra. "Shut that door, Miguel. Don't want anybody coming in here. And take his gun."

He jerked his head at Shay, and started down the hall to the cells. In the runway, he looked closely at Lund, then shifted his gaze to the adjoining cage. Sierra joined them; he leaned against the door frame, his swarthy features expressionless, his dark eyes filled with a quiet reserve.

125

"Maybe," Cole said to Shay, "you'd better be telling me what this's all about."

Jim went through his story, beginning with the shooting of Gilman, then his escape, his stumbling onto Cal Garrick, and his subsequent visit to Stella. He told of Barndollar and the rancher's death at the hands of the Apaches, his return to the Slausson farm, and all that had taken place thereafter. When he had finished, he sagged against the wall of the runway, short of breath and weak. Cole faced Lund through the bars. "What do you say to this, mister?"

"He's a goddam liar," the outlaw said flatly. "Sun's got him, that's what. He's crazy, plumb crazy, cooking up a yarn like that."

The lawman regarded Lund with a secretive, thin contempt, and transferred his attention to the girl. "Figured you'd be in here sooner or later, Stella, but not for something like this. What've you got to say?"

Stella, sitting on the edge of her cot, shook her head. "Dave's doing the talking."

"Dave's got plenty of trouble of his own. You better be thinking something up."

Jim Shay raised an eyebrow.

"Meaning what by that?" Lund demanded.

"Meaning Rue didn't die—leastwise not right off. We found him. He was barely alive. Those small-caliber bullets bleed a man to death slow. He told us what had happened, said you and this Sanford shot him. He died here in town this morning."

"That was Sanford—not me!" Lund shouted immediately. "The deputy had me chained to a tree when Sanford opened up on him with a pocket gun. Ask Shay—he seen it all."

Cole, again facing Lund, said, "You denying what Shay says about the Slaussons?"

"You're damned right I am! Fact is, I ain't never heard of them. Maybe I was there when Aaron blasted the deputy, but that's all you got on me."

"Same go for you, Stella?"

"She ain't no guiltier than me, Sheriff. That's the God's truth. Now, how about letting us out of here? We ain't had no sleep or nothing to eat—"

George Cole looked down. "No hurry, Lund. You're in there

for Gilman's murder, and I'll be finding out more about this Garrick killing. We'll get you something to eat."

He turned to Jim. His thin face looked tired. And stern.

"Ain't much you've given me to go on, Shay. Only your word against theirs, far as the Slausson killings are concerned. And you being a convicted criminal before the law, I'd have no luck getting the court to accept your word—"

"He tells the truth, Sheriff."

At Miguel Sierra's calm pronouncement, the old lawman whirled about. Shay pulled himself up straight. In the hush that followed voices in the street could be heard clearly.

"I hear them talk."

"You heard who talk?" Cole shouted. "When? Why the hell didn't you say something sooner?"

"Only now do I have a chance," Sierra said, unruffled by the lawman's impatience. "I go to the store for a sack of Bull. I return but I hear talking. I wonder who has come so I listen by the window. I hear this Lund tell Shay he is a big fool to wait for you, he say there is no proof—"

"You goddam lousy Mex!" Lund yelled, surging to the front of his cell. "If I could get my hands—"

"It is this man who murdered the old Slaussons. This I know. The girl, she is mix up in it—"

"You never heard me say I done it!" Lund raged. "Was Aaron that strung up the old man. I was only—"

The outlaw's voice trailed off. He swore, shook his head, and fell back onto his cot. Jim Shay moved toward the door.

"Reckon that lets me out," he murmured. "You want me, I'll be at the hotel." He braced himself with one hand against the wall.

"Fine," Cole said. "Likely be needing a statement of some kind for the judge. I'll send your gear over."

Shay nodded woodenly. He paused before Sierra, thrust out his arm. "Obliged to you, *amigo*."

"*Con mucho gusto,*" Sierra said, and winked slyly.

Shay frowned, but before he could say more, George Cole's voice cut through the quiet. "See that nobody out there in the street bothers him, Miguel. And find out where he was when he shot Sanford. We'll be going after him—or his body."

The deputy bobbed his head. Shay had not moved; he still looked at the dark, inscrutable face of the Mexican, trying to read the secret in the depths of his eyes. Sierra grinned, showing his gleaming white teeth.

"I think you could use a couple of drinks, maybe."

Jim nodded. "I could—but I'm wondering—"

The deputy lifted his hand quickly, pushed Shay gently into the corridor and toward the door. "No questions, *amigo*," he said softly. "Sometimes it is necessary to—how you say— prime the pump. There let it end and speak no more of it. *Comprende?*"

A tired smile crossed Jim Shay's haggard face. "*Comprendo*," he said, and moved on.

Ray Hogan is an author who has inspired a loyal following over the years since he published his first Western novel *Ex-Marshal* in 1956. Hogan was born in Willow Springs, Missouri, where his father was town marshal. At five the Hogan family moved to Albuquerque where Ray Hogan still lives in the foothills of the Sandia and Manzano mountains. His father was on the Albuquerque police force and, in later years, owned the Overland Hotel. It was while listening to his father and other old-timers tell tales from the past that Ray was inspired to recast these tales in fiction. From the beginning he did exhaustive research into the history and the people of the Old West and the walls of his study are lined with various firearms, spurs, pictures, books, and memorabilia, about all of which he can talk in dramatic detail. Among his most popular works are the series of books about Shawn Starbuck, a searcher in quest for a lost brother who has a clear sense of right and wrong and who is willing to stand up and be counted when it is a question of fairness or justice. His other major series is about lawman John Rye whose reputation has earned him the sobriquet The Doomsday Marshal. "I've attempted to capture the courage and bravery of those men and women that lived out West and the dangers and problems they had to overcome," Hogan once remarked. If his lawmen protagonists seem sometimes larger than life, it is because they are men of integrity, heroes who through grit of character and common sense are able to overcome the obstacles they encounter despite often overwhelming odds. This same grit of character can also be found in Hogan's heroines and in *The Vengeance of Fortuna West* Hogan wrote a gripping and totally believable account of a woman who takes up the badge and tracks the men who killed her lawman husband by ambush. No less intriguing in her way is Nellie Dupray, convicted of rustling in *The Glory Trail*. Above all, what is most impressive about Hogan's Western novels is the consistent quality with which each is crafted, the compelling depth of his characters, and his ability to juxtapose the complexities of human conflict into narratives always as intensely interesting as they are emotionally involving. His latest novel is *Soldier in Buckskin*, published as a **Five Star Western**.